Code Name:

Iron Spear

1941

Published by South Branch Scribbler
Dieppe, New Brunswick
Canada

eBook ISBN – 978-1-988291-23-9
Paperback ISBN – 978-1-988291-22-2

Also by Allan Hudson

Historical fiction
Father
The Alexanders Vol. 1 1911 -1920

The Jo Naylor Series
Shattered Figurine
Shattered Lives
Shattered Dreams

Short Stories
A Box of Memories

The Drake Alexander Series
Dark Side of a Promise
Wall of War
Vigilantes

Anthologies
Autumn Paths
Winter Paths

To Gloria. My one true love.

Royal Canadian Air Force Station Scoudouc
1941

The body was headless, it had no fingers.
Identification would be difficult, if not impossible.

1

October 6th Monday

The roar of an airplane taking off echoes through the fields. A Tiger Moth rises into the glare of the yellow lip cresting on the horizon. The huge hangars of the Scoudouc Air Force Base are muted silhouettes on the skyline giving no evidence of the sounds of hundreds of men and women waking up and going to work. Tim Grant stands astride a borrowed bicycle shielding his eyes from the rising sun to watch the plane veer off to the north on what's likely a training flight. It's the main occupation at the air base from what he hears. There are lots of British gents and some from New Zealand with their funny accents around these days. Air Force people from all over Canada too. Teaching them how to fly. He'd like to fly a plane, viewing things all tiny from above. He glances down at his bum ankle, casting blame, and knows it will never happen.

Tim took off early with his little brother's bicycle, his first day off from his crazy shifts at the store in seven days. He doesn't have to be back until Saturday. He's standing at the gate where the Air Force put up their *No Trespassing* sign and he waits out of sight behind a cluster of trees. His best friend, Pierre, is supposed to join him this morning. He said he'd meet him here at the gate at 6:30, daybreak, and they'd sneak in together. It's almost seven and with no sign of his friend, he's not waiting any longer. Pierre may have changed his mind. He enters the wooded area leading to the fields.

He's doing some end of season fishing. There are still trout in the brook. He knows he's not supposed to be on this land, expropriated by the government to build the base and continue expanding. But he's been coming all summer and nothing has happened yet. The road in is the one used before the farmers stopped working the soil; tall dead grass covers most of the fields now. His last days off were over two weeks ago when he asked for an extra day to move into his new apartment. His friends all teased him about living at home, too old at twenty to be under his momma's wings. He laughs to himself thinking that all he owns is a bed, a small table and two chairs. He has a lot of work to do, and he has to remember to pick up some bread on his way home. The milkman, Mr. Doucet, called out from his van to him earlier, thinking it was his brother.

"Hey Donnie boy, you must be up to no good if you're awake this early?"

Then he drove off with both chins wiggling at his own humour. It's no wonder. Folks say he and his brother look so much alike. Donnie's a few inches shorter, tall for a sixteen-year-old. Same curly hair always looking unkempt, same color as their mother's, the halfway point between blond and brunette, like caramel. Strong chins and wide jaw. Their eyes are different, Donnie's a frivolous blue and Tim's a serious brown.

He parks the bike under a cluster of alders at the edge of the field near the road he pedaled in on. Using the thin trees lining the brook to hide behind, he carries his rod and a creel hung over one shoulder and makes his way toward the wooded area where a deep hole exists. The fishing is best where it bubbles out to a shallower area. When he nears the tree line, he hesitates and gets a mild scare when he sees movement off to his left twenty feet away from the waterway. Someone disappeared behind a large pine tree which looks older than his grandfather, thick and heavy branched. Looking down, he sees trodden patches of grass, not heavily used but obvious. It makes him look at his own trail. He didn't notice any disturbance on his way in. Curiosity gets the best of him; he wonders who would be in the woods so early. His eyes dart everywhere. Treading on the balls of his feet he moves toward where he saw the movement.

No one will know he's missing until he doesn't show up for work.

2

October 6th 6:45 pm

The man gloats at himself in the mirror. He's still under control and on schedule. It was a stupid place to bury the transmitter but not his to worry why, only that it was where he was told it would be. He only hopes his decoy covers his tracks for the next four days. The sub will pick him up in the Northumberland Strait off the coast of Cap-de-Cocagne, at their prearranged time

Staring at his image, he wears the fisherman's clothes. He had no choice; the others were too small. A plaid jacket covers the blood-stained shirt where the knife went in. The pants needed to be rolled up and are too tight in the thighs. The black and red rubber boots that pinch his toes are left at the door.

He empties the pockets: wallet with no money, a bone handled jackknife, sixty-three cents and a lifesaver covered with lint. He'll destroy the wallet and throw the lifesaver in the garbage. He sets his own things aside - his knife, phony papers, a car key and another key a size smaller. He finally got rid of the damn tag of the car key. He knows he shouldn't be carrying the smaller key but worries about leaving it somewhere, so he keeps it with him at all times. He shucks the clothes off and into a ball on the floor to burn later. Standing naked in front of a full-length mirror, he reflects on his physique. For a man his age, he's in good shape, still strong, no extra fat.

Heading into the shower, his only regret is losing one of his best disguises. But he still has the most important one. Remembering that disguise, a moment of panic besets him, almost like a chill. Going back to the dresser where he put his own things, he searches through them for an important piece of paper. It's not there. He curses in his mother tongue.

"*Scheiße.*"

Going back to the balled-up clothing, he digs through the pockets once more and finds them empty. He's not sure what to do. His plan calls for the other uniform. It was all wrinkled in a package when he received it in the mail. There was no return address so he has no idea where it came from, only that he was told it was coming. He needs it to be perfect. When he dropped it off at the cleaners, he decided to leave it there until he needed it. He figured it to be the safest place to hide it. He used a phony name and even though he remembers it well enough, without the stub, he'll be asked for ID, and he has none. He destroyed it.

He sits on the edge of the bed, thinking. Forgetting his wallet at home is logical enough and if he needs to, he'll exert his authority and military duty - embarrass them. He'll retrieve the uniform as soon as can. Carry on as usual, then strike.

The dumb fisherman is the first man he's killed since being activated, but it's unlikely to be the last. If he dies himself in his attempt, it will have been for the Fuhrer. Heil Hitler!

3

October 7th 3:25 pm

Aircraftsman Second Class (AC2) Jeremy Carter and Flight Sergeant (FS) Wilbur Booth are standing at ease in front of Group Captain (GC) Braydon Clark. Clark's stare lets both men know he's not happy about being interrupted. Carter is not at ease. His knees wobble. His upper lip shines from nervous anticipation. He has to grip his sweaty hands firmly behind his back to stop them from slipping out. He waits for a reply from Clark, eyes three inches above his head. He wishes he wasn't here.

Booth stares directly ahead. He knows enough to be quiet under his superior's steely gaze. Booth grins inwardly, knowing Clark rarely stands up in his presence as he's not a lot over the barest minimum, a good nine inches shorter than Clark's six-foot three frame. He's obviously not a fighting man but one better suited to administration. Bald head, thick glasses, a pot belly, he'd not be mistaken for anything other than a desk jockey. But as he outranks everyone else, he's the boss.

Clark takes off his glasses and scrutinizes the men at attention in front of him, eyes glued to the wall behind him. He's familiar with Booth's rocky jaw and big frame and hates his good looks and thick shoulders. The other one is a kid, still has pimples and could do with putting on some weight, but his eyes show promise. He smells like a new recruit.

"What is it, Sergeant? Be quick, I'm busy with this report."

Booth turns to AC2 Carter.

"Tell him, Carter."

"Sir. I was doing clean-up duty along the edge of the brook in back of the station and I found a body. A dead body."

Clark sighs heavily. He feels like the ceiling just fell on him. His shoulders sag with the news. This is not something he needs. He only took over this post three months ago, and his first thought is about himself and how to handle this situation. It's not going to be good to have the police crawling around with a top-secret section on the base.

"Civilian or military?"

"The corpse is wearing the dress uniform of the Canadian Air Force. The insignia on the sleeve is that of leading aircraftsman."

"Any idea who it is?"

Carter looks to his Sergeant, who nods for him to go ahead.

"No, Sir. It's impossible to tell."

Clark is taken aback. He sits back in his chair, fiddling with the pen he was writing with.

"How so?"

"The cadaver has no head."

Clark shudders at the image and shakes his head with his lips pursed. The men know not to interrupt. They watch him in deep thought tapping his pen on the desk and see he is clearly disturbed. He looks to the sergeant.

"Who else knows about this?"

"No one, Sir. Carter came directly to me, and I deemed it important enough to come directly to you."

"Well done, Sergeant. Where's the body?"

He's looking at Carter whose Adam's apple is bobbing, sweat beading on his forehead.

"It's... it's still where I found it, Sir."

"All right then. Give me a minute, Gentlemen."

Clark stares at the pages he was writing on. He's trying to decide the best way to approach the problem. After five minutes, he addresses Carter. Perspiration is running down the side of the young man's face.

The GC passes him a box of tissues from the side of the desk.

"Relax Carter. Here. Wipe your brow."

Carter does so and stands easy once more.

"I am keeping you under special detail, Carter, and until I say different, you will work with Sergeant Booth on this. But I want to be very, very clear on what I am going to say to you. Do not mention this to anyone on or off the base until I say so. Is that clear?"

"Yes Sir! Very clear."

"If I or the Sergeant hear of you telling anyone until this is cleared up or the police take over, I will make sure you spend the rest of your military career in the stockade. Is *that* clear?"

Louder now.

"Yes Sir!"

"Wait in the outer office, Carter."

The young airman snaps to attention, salutes, and leaves.

"All right, Sergeant. Let's try to clear this up on our own. I don't think our superiors would want civilians or police on the premises. You know what's going on here. Our need for secrecy is paramount. Do you agree?"

"Yes, Sir!"

"Very well. I want you and Carter to retrieve the body, but not until after dark tonight. Number 5 hangar is underutilized at present. If I remember correctly, the storerooms or offices are not being used at all. Is that correct?"

"Yes Sir."

"Place the body inside one of those rooms for now. Use one of the workbenches. Select sentries you know to follow orders and have them deny passage to the inner rooms. No one, besides you and I or anyone without my approval, are to be granted entrance regardless of rank. Have a rotating shift set up for the next three days. Give them strict orders not to be nosy or they will receive the same punishment that I promised Carter."

"What about the smell, Sir? I don't know how long the body has been there or exposed but I'm guessing it happened recently."

"We should wait until we have someone on it. Let's lock this up for 72 hours and see if we can figure out what is going on."

"Yes sir."

Clark checks his watch to see it is almost four o'clock, meaning a shift change in a few minutes.

"Who was the gentleman that cracked the problem with unexplained inventory shortages at the Moncton Air Force base?"

"That would be Warrant Officer First Class Stefan Kravchenko."

"Kravchenko? Want kind of surname is that?"

"Ukrainian, Sir. Third generation Canadian. Former police officer from Winnipeg."

"How do you know this, Sergeant?"

"Went through boot camp with him, Sir. We both joined up in the spring of '40."

"Do you know where he is now?"

"Yes, Sir. He's stationed at Royal Canadian Air Force Detachment Saint John. They coordinate all Air Force Service Police action for New Brunswick out of the Milledgeville airport."

"Ah yes, of course. I believe Wing Commander Henderson is the commanding officer there. I'll get Kravchenko transferred ASAP. You, Carter, and he will work on this together. Make yourself available to him and I don't need to remind you that this is hush-hush, Sergeant, do I?"

"No Sir!"

"We will all meet at the storeroom of Hangar No. 5 at oh-seven-hundred hours tomorrow morning. Dismissed."

The sergeant snaps to attention, gives a sharp about face and leaves. With no other choice, Clark gets on the phone to his subordinate in Saint John.

4

5:23 pm

WO1 Kravchenko is eating at the mess when he receives an urgent message from WC Henderson to see him at once. Leaving his half-eaten meal, he dons his hat and leaves for the commander's office. The message is quick and simple.

"Pack enough gear for 72 hours and report to GC Clark at Canadian Air Force Base Scoudouc before 07:00 tomorrow. It's best if you leave as soon as possible. Draw a vehicle from the carpool. Once there, you are to contact FS Booth who will be expecting you. Ask for him at the gate."

"May I ask why, Sir?"

"Your guess is as good as mine, Kravchenko. They didn't tell me. It was an order. Carry on."

Kravchenko is young to be a warrant officer. He's not the youngest in the Canadian Forces but at thirty-five, he has an impressive list of accomplishments as a member of the service police. He refused the opportunity to enlist as a commissioned officer wanting to work with the non-com personnel. His rapid rise through the ranks is contributed to Air Marshal Benning, after Kravchenko discovered and busted the German sympathizers that sabotaged the runway at RCAF Station Rivers in Manitoba.

His friends always tease him that with his good looks, he could've been a poster boy. Taller than average, he's squarely built. He's a man who thinks before he speaks; his eyes question everything. Because of his no-nonsense attitude, he is often mistaken for a dour person when he's in a serious mood. That hides a more genial person, one who likes cold beer, children, good books, and pretty ladies. Although single, he's had a long-time relationship with his high school sweetheart, a nurse stationed in England. No one is certain how involved they are but he's never been labelled as a womanizer, always a gentleman except when it comes to ruffians or rude and ignorant people.

Leaving the air base in Saint John in a 1939 Dodge coupe painted a drab olive with a *Service Police* decal in the back window, he realizes he won't get to Scoudouc before midnight. He hopes the sergeant is still available at that late hour as he needs to get some rest and be sharp for whatever tomorrow morning brings him.

5

October 8th 6:29 am

Kravchenko has been sleeping in one of the barracks Booth provided for him. After a quick coffee and toast, Sergeant Booth is accompanying him to Hangar Number Five. Kravchenko has been filled in with what Booth already knows. Other than the body, its condition and its movement to the hangar, there is very little to tell him. He advises Kravchenko that GC Clark will be updating him shortly on the need for privacy.

"I wish I had seen the body in situ. Sometimes clues can be picked up at the site."

"I don't know for certain, but I don't think the location where Carter found him is where he was murdered."

"What makes you say that Sergeant?"

"There was no sign of a scuffle or trodden grass anywhere near the corpse other than Carter's. I checked the immediate area for anything odd, being careful where I stepped."

"Did anyone check the waterway above or below?"

"No, Sir, we didn't. It was too dark, and we were under orders to get the body to Hangar Five at nightfall."

Kravchenko is thinking things through when they arrive at the hanger. Pallets of plane parts, dry goods and two maintenance trucks fill the front area inside the cavernous building. The hood is open on one of the trucks and two men are tinkering at the engine. The smell of grease from the packing boxes and a faint odor of diesel fuel gives the air a mechanical scent. A storage facility, offices and lunchroom are situated in the back part. An area twenty feet in front of the rooms is barricaded off by eight-foot sawhorses the whole width of the building. An armed LAC is stationed in a gap of three feet in the middle.

LAC Langley stands at attention and salutes. Sergeant Booth introduces Kravchenko, telling him he will come and go. Kravchenko voluntarily opens his soft sided briefcase for the LAC to inspect. He nods, barely giving it a glance.

"Thank you, Sir."

Leaving the LAC as he was, they enter the hallway which extends for thirty feet where it splits into a T, with similar hallways left and right. None of the rooms are occupied. A larger room, back right corner, is where the body is stored. Sergeant Booth leads the way. Upon entering the room, both men are surprised to find GC Clark there standing over the body. He acknowledges the men returning their salutes.

"Good morning, Gentlemen. You must be Kravchenko?"

"Yes, Sir. I'm at your disposal until you no longer need me."

"Good. I wanted to meet with you, of course. But I also need to warn you that there are activities within the base that must be kept secret. I'm not sure if they may be the cause of this individual's death. So therefore, I'm keeping this on the base for the next ...let me see...today is Wednesday. So you have until Friday morning to solve this or we will have no choice but to go to the police."

Kravchenko is staring at the body laid out on a steel workbench and squints his nose at the odour already permeating the room as the body begins to decompose.

"May I ask what the big secret is, Sir?"

"Yes, I believe it is imperative to your investigation. As you may know, RCAF Coverdale, near Moncton, is part of the Canada/United States Atlantic High Frequency Direction Finding Network, responsible for direction finding coordination for Atlantic Search and Rescue operations. Here at Scoudouc, we are in receipt of a new cavity magnetron and associated paraphernalia, created in England, still early in its development. It's being set up to test direction finding in the microwave spectrum in hopes it will be much more effective. The decision was made to carry out the trials here it here supposedly far away from spies. We will be working with RCAF Coverdale to test the effectiveness of the magnetron."

Kravchenko is well aware of the different bases using direction finding in defense, rescue, and support of the country. Nova Scotia has three if he remembers correctly. Those would be the obvious choice as they are surrounded by water and unobstructed airspace. But too obvious, he surmises. Scoudouc is a wiser choice.

Kravchenko commits Clark's words to memory and the words "spies" causes him to ponder. New Brunswick seems an unlikely place for the Nazi hierarchy to be concerned with. Such drama doesn't make sense in his books, of course, the "secret part", the very word is a lure, nectar for the enemy.

"Is this a large object? Can a man or woman carry it?"

"Oh yes. The magnetron itself is no bigger than one of your lower arms. No good on its own but in conjunction with the proper construction, it is a valuable resource. It would not do for it to get into the wrong hands."

"I will certainly consider this in my investigation, Group Captain. If I may, Sir, have you considered extra security on the location and if so, perhaps try not to make it too obvious at this point, keep everything looking normal."

"We've already considered that. Sergeant, see to the warrant officer's advice for deployment."

"Yes, Sir."

Kravchenko points to the body.

"I'd like to look now, if I may?"

Before Clark can answer, the door opens to admit Carter. Clark speaks to all three men, glaring at each directly.

"We four are the only ones on base to know what is happening. Be sure to keep it that way."

The three of them stand erect, chests out and their response, which couldn't have been better if they'd practiced, sings out in harmony.

"Yes Sir, Group Captain, Sir."

He leaves and the men move closer. After introductions, Kravchenko has Carter relate when he found the body.

"It was shortly after three o'clock yesterday afternoon. I discovered it in the marsh behind the hangars, near the small stream that flows toward the village and eventually empties into Shediac Bay. The only thing in the water were the feet."

Kravchenko is examining the body closely, paying attention to the portion of the neck sticking out of the collar. The skin is curled in where the head has been severed, the edges ragged. Same as the metatarsals on the hands. The fingers have been crudely cut above the second knuckle.

Looking close at the dress shirt, he examines the collar and cuffs.

"I think this uniform was put on the body after it was dismembered."

The sergeant looks curiously at Kravchenko.

"How can you tell, Sir?"

"There are no stains on the collar or cuffs and if he was wearing this when killed or decapitated, it should be covered in blood. It's too neat. Let's be careful and get the clothing off. Lay it out on the bench next to the wall. We can look at those later."

The men shift the body around until it lies naked on the bench. Due to livor mortis, the skin is pale blue and blotchy. He's seen enough dead bodies to estimate this cadaver is approximately two days old, still in the early stage of decomposition, autolysis. It has not begun to bloat but with the gasses building up it will be soon. He notes that insect activity has taken place with blowfly eggs already present. Blowflies are usually the first insect to arrive, followed by flesh flies and beetles, mostly within the first twenty-four hours.

"If you discovered the body yesterday afternoon, it was likely put there early yesterday morning or late the night before. That would be my guess."

Rigor mortis has stiffened some of the joints, particularly the knees which are drawn up toward the chest. Kravchenko inspects the lividity, the purplish red discoloration along the back, buttocks, and thighs where the blood has pooled. The most obvious detail is the knife wound below the ribcage directly under the heart, a professional stroke with a long sharp knife. He examines every wrinkle and every pore with steely patience. The other men are impressed with his attention to the corpse. He makes note of something else when he's inspecting the feet. The skin is puckered from being in the water, but he can see the left foot is disfigured at the ankle likely from a break not properly set. There's a mole the size of a dime on the back left shoulder. Otherwise there are no other scars or injuries, no signs of other operations. He estimates the man to be close to six feet tall and approximately 180 pounds. He is uncertain of the age but from the texture of the skin, he estimates it at younger than thirty.

Moving on to the clothing, Carter goes through the pockets and sets the items next to the jacket. It's the typical blue of the air force uniform. The shoulder patches have the curved Canada patch at the top with the eagle immediately under it, and the propeller patch of a LAC. Other than mud off the cuffs of the trousers and sodden boots, there's not much to see. There is neither a wallet nor ID. Kravchenko is looking at a comb, several coins and a soiled handkerchief, when he notices Carter digging in the trouser pocket.

"There's something stuck in here, where the pocket is sown together in the corner. Ah, I got it."

Cater hands a tightly folded receipt from Sunrise Drycleaners in Moncton dated three weeks previously. Only the last name is visible - Coleman. When Carter sees the name, he has a big grin.

"There, we know who it is. We just need to look for a missing Coleman."

"It's possible but I doubt that's who this is. Whoever did this, went to a lot of trouble removing the head and fingers and any ID. They wouldn't have overlooked this. It might've been planted there to throw us off. We'll definitely follow it up though."

He scans the cadaver once more. Finding nothing else of interest, Kravchenko asks Carter to take him to the place where he found the body.

6

7:44 am

Leaving by the back emergency exit, they cross the street, walk past the barracks, cross another dirt road and then an open field. It takes them ten minutes until they come to the small stream that defines the edge of the property. Carter shows Kravchenko where the body was lying. The marsh is soft below their feet. The alders lining the stream are all wearing their lemon-coloured autumn leaves. Pointing to a spot where the bushes are separated by a fallen log, Carter explains what he found.

"It was on the other side of this old log. I only noticed it because the arm was resting against the log with the hand sticking up and it looked like a one of those big mushrooms that grows out of old trees. But then I saw a piece of blue uniform that didn't look natural. So I checked it out and there it was. The boots were in the water up to the ankles, the rest close to the log."

Kravchenko squats near the log, using it for support while he studies the terrain. The marsh grasses are flattened. He can see the drag marks of the feet when the men pulled the body away last night. He regrets not seeing the body when it was lying here. There are several footprints in the soft soil by the water line, and two indentations which look like heel prints. There's too much disturbance after the scene to know if anything is relevant. Seeing nothing else, he walks to the edge of the water and looks upstream, to the west. He'd call it bigger than a brook, certainly not a river, maybe an average of fifteen or sixteen feet wide. There's a lazy rhythm to the flow, shallow along the edges and an unhurried channel from a source beyond the air base. Fields on both sides are soldiered by a fleet of yellowing young birch and evergreens until the watercourse disappears into a forest of hardwoods wearing their autumn bonnets. Kravchenko turns to the Sergeant.

"What are those lands on the other side of the brook?"

"Those fields have been fallow since the war, unfarmed and off limits to civilians. Expropriated."

"Cause any angry residents?"

"No, Sir. Oddly enough the community is one hundred percent behind us. They're quick to let us know if anything funny goes on around the place. Mostly false alarms."

"I can't see any houses or farms."

"The water in front of us is running to the east. The main road you came in on before the street to the base, runs north and south as does the village. So after the fields it is more forest again."

"I expect there would be an access road to the fields for them to be tended."

"Yes, there is. It's gated. The service police and select personnel have keys. I personally haven't seen it or even have time to look. I'm from Saskatchewan, have never been east of Ontario before and don't get much time for sightseeing, Sir."

Kravchenko looks to Carter who is standing a step beyond the sergeant, wide eyed, with curiosity all over his face.

"What about you, AC2 Carter?"

"Yes, Sir. I hung out with guy from Scoudouc a couple of summers. Helped them bring in their hay. I know where the road is."

"Good. What happens downstream?"

"It bends to the north and loops around the front of the base. You crossed it on the road in. Then it runs east again to the bay. On the street into the base and before you get to the main gate, there's a dirt road along a short stretch of the brook that ends at an old sawmill, abandoned during the depression. Our security personnel check it out occasionally on regular patrols."

Kravchenko studies the ground again but doesn't find anything he might've missed first glance. Satisfied, he turns to the men.

"Sergeant Booth. Could you search this side of the brook up to the forested area and watch for recent broken limbs or crushed grass, anything which looks like activity in the last forty-eight hours. Carter, you do the same but in the opposite direction and when you get to the road to the sawmill, cross over and loop back this way. I'm going to wade through and work my way toward the woods on the opposite side."

After crossing the stream, cold water seeping into his boots, Kravchenko finds the crumpled grass of footprints going along the brook. Ten minutes later he finds evidence of a lot of movement near the tree line. The grass is disturbed by something large having been dragged from the woods to the water's edge. The body likely. Whoever did it, must've moved the body down the stream in the water. Why? Where was he taking it? And how did it end up where it was found? Moving back to the trodden area he first discovered, he sees crushed grass and footprints leading into the trees behind a large pine tree.

Ten steps in, is a narrow clearing. Blood covered twigs, pine needles and leaves make an eerie sight. A pair of what could have been welder's gloves, all blood stained, are tossed under bushes near a hole. It is at least three feet square and over a foot deep where something has been dug up. Soil is piled to the right of the opening. Kravchenko rubs his chin in contemplation of what might've been there. It would have to be something of significance if it was worth killing over. He's disturbed by a shout from Booth.

"Sir, are you there? You need to see this!"

Kravchenko is drawn to the urgency in the voice and rushes back out to the brook where he hears Sergeant Booth calling from a short distance downstream on the other side.

"I'm on my way, Sergeant."

He has to push aside a tangle of young trees and step over dead wood for a dozen feet from the edge of the brook. He can see Booth on the other side by a larger fir tree with one side of its thick roots sticking in the stream; the water's slowly chewing the earth away. When Booth sees Kravchenko, he points to the cluster of the roots with their tendrils sticking out in the stream like ghostly arms with no hands.

It's hard to make anything out as the water waves and bubbles when it flows over the twisted roots. He zeros in on an unusually white object. Bobbing in the current, impaled upon a broken root, is a head.

7

Kravchenko points to the tangled roots.

"Can you retrieve it, Sergeant? Use your jacket."

"I'll try."

Booth kneels at the edge of the tree and lays on his chest with his shoulders over the water. With his face scrunched in distaste, he reaches down with his jacket and scoops it up, then brings the arms of the jacket together to enclose the head securely and pull it from the stream.

"I've got it."

"Keep it wrapped and take it back to where we have the body. It's too deep for me to wade across here and I want to find out if Carter found anything useful. I'll join you as soon as I can. Thank you, Sergeant."

"Yes, Sir."

Kravchenko makes his way down stream and meets Carter moving in his direction on the same side. They meet almost across from where the body was first found.

"Did you find something, Carter?"

"Nothing unusual, Sir."

"All right then, let's go across and meet Sergeant Booth. He found a missing piece."

"A missing piece, Sir?"

"The head."

Carter stiffens and sucks in his breath.

"Whoa. In the water?"

"Yes."

"That ain't going to be pretty... Sir."

"No, it's not."

◻

Carter shows the warrant officer where they can cross with only getting their boots wet, not over the tops. They're back across the fields and through the barracks area and have to go around to the front of the hangar. Entering the regular door, they are greeted inside by LAC Robichaud standing security in the front of even more sawhorses. Gone are the trucks, mechanics, and petroleum stink. LAC Langley is still on duty at the opening through the inner sawhorses and clears the men with Robichaud, who salutes and stands aside. Clark has doubled up on security, keeping it quiet.

In the makeshift morgue, Flight Sergeant Booth has the head lying on another steel bench adjacent to the body. His jacket lies under it. Kravchenko peers down at the white bloated flesh, disfigured from fish or eels feeding on it. The eyes are missing. Other features are swollen beyond anything familiar. It can only be defined by its nostrils, exposed teeth and one remaining brow. A cap of short hair is plastered to the scalp, shaved on the sides with no facial hair.

"There's a lot of damage to it. There's certainly nothing identifiable about it."

He has to step back and waves to clear the air. The mortifying body is beginning to swell from gathering gases.

"Sergeant. I need you and Carter to get this on ice somehow or to put very cold water under it. Rig something up. After that, I need you to go to the supply depot to see if any uniforms have been stolen or gone missing. Check with all LACs on base for the same. If there's nothing here, try the next nearest bases, Salisbury, Coverdale, Fredericton, and

Saint John for now. We may have to do a more extensive search later. Check for anyone on leave, sick, missing and so on. Get names and possible whereabouts."

Remembering the dry-cleaning stub, he adds another directive.

"And check for all possible Colemans on any of the bases you contact."

Yes, Sir."

"What I need you to do Carter, is to get a camera. The Public Affairs people on base will have a photographer or have one on notice. Commandeer whatever you need with GC Clark's authority. You get any hassle, get me involved. Then go to where you found the body. Don't disturb the site but get a dozen or so shots from different angles. Especially all the footprints. You with me so far, Carter?"

Carter perk ups as if he had a coffee buzz, and rubs his hands together, eyes bulging with exuberance.

"Oh yes, Sir. I understand completely... Sir."

Kravchenko grins at Carter's enthusiasm and likes the man.

"Good, then follow the brook on the side where we met earlier, and you will see where the grass is disturbed over to a thick pine tree. There was something buried there but I didn't get a chance to look closely. I'm going back there now, and I want you to take photos of the scene. So, get a camera and meet me there first. Do the others after."

"Right away, Sir."

AC2 Carter gives a quick salute. Full of spit, he is excited to be included in the investigation, part of the secret: a dead man with no head, and then a head. He can't even begin to try to explain the energy he's feeling. It's even better than the first time he went up in a plane. He asks the sergeant about the ice and before they leave on their chilling exercise, Kravchenko raises a finger to the sergeant.

"Yes, Sir?"

"Give the GC a quick update, will you, Sergeant. Then you and Carter are done here."

"Yes, Sir."

Kravchenko glances at the pale head. There is something bothering him about it. He studies it once more, especially the wound, then returns to the cadaver to compare its neck wound. He sees it right away. A chill of dread climbs up his spine and the hairs on the back of his neck bristle. Both remains have an Adam's apple.

8

Kravchenko's shock is diverted by the click of the door opening. He turns to see GC Clark enter. Clark stalls when he sees the warrant officer's pale face and look of bewilderment.

"What is it Kravchenko?"

"It's worse than we thought, Group Captain."

Clark hastens to the worktable to see the body Kravchenko is pointing to.

"Look at the neck."

Clark has his hands behind his back and bends to look. He is able to bear it but still feels the revulsion he had when he first saw it.

"What am I looking for, Kravchenko?"

He directs Clark to the lump near the cut.

"Ah yes, the Adam's apple."

Clark looks to Kravchenko with brows raised.

"And?"

Kravchenko steps back so Clark can see the head on the still wet jacket. He hasn't seen it yet. It's the first chance he's had to get away from his desk since the sergeant apprised him. He steps closer and stops a stride away. The face is grotesque and waterlogged. He notices the cut has rough edges. He fears that his breakfast will escape and gags at the horrid sight. Kravchenko is sympathetic with the GC's squeamishness. He knows the feeling.

"Look here, Sir, one quick glance where my finger is."

Clark forces his focus back to the finger and slowly to where it directs him. He physically jolts back from the revelation and shudders.

"Good Lord. How ghastly!"

He turns away swallowing the bile in his throat and looks to Kravchenko.

"Now we have two dead people. What's your next step?"

"With all due respect, Sir, do you not think we should contact the police?

Clark sticks his chin out, his hands behind his back once more. He worries about this going public.

"As I said earlier, Warrant Officer, you have until Friday morning before we contact the police. I believe, from your credentials, your investigation would be no less effective than our regular police department. I have every confidence in you to find the answers. We can keep this in our own backyard so to speak."

"But the victims may be civilians, Sir."

"We don't know that for certain, do we Kravchenko? Found with a uniform, close to an Air Force base. My first guess is to look for a missing airman... or two."

Kravchenko knows there is no arguing with him, and orders are orders. He is not too concerned about keeping the bodies secret. It will be an impossibility. Clark set him on this chase, and he'll see it through. And whatever he finds out will help the police. He knows the drill. His mentor back in Winnipeg, Detective Chornovil, was one of the best snoops he ever met. Try and think like the bad guy. Go with your gut. Keep looking and find something in common.

9

Kravchenko crosses the brook below where the body was found. He goes in the direction he sent Carter earlier where he plans to intensely study the terrain. Not that he doesn't trust Carter, but he wants to be certain the man didn't miss anything. The road into the fields is visible to his right. Checking it out, he walks for fifty feet and seeing nothing, turns back. Walking toward the brook again, the sun is behind him, he catches a glint of something shining by the cluster of trees separating the fields and the forest next to it. Going closer, he finds a bicycle. He doesn't touch it and looks for anything odd. Finding nothing noticeable, he digs it out from under the bushes and stands it by him on the road. It's a large bike, maybe a twenty-eight inch, red with white trim and chain guard. One hand grip on the handlebars has a stream of red and white plastic strips flowing from it and the other doesn't. Seeing it has a kickstand, he extends it down and leaves the bike.

Nearing the bend in the brook, he finds the dirt road leading to the abandoned sawmill. He walks up onto the road and looks in both directions. To his right, he can make out a hillock of sawdust with the top of its cone rising above the forest canopy, the dilapidated building hidden by trees. He estimates it to be about five hundred feet from where he is standing.

To his left, the road runs for several hundred feet before joining the main entrance to the base. The brook flows under it and sweeps to the left where it follows the road for a ways before swinging under it again. There are many tire tracks. The only things distinguishable are some tracks that pull close to the side and stop. Nothing unusual or telling in those.

Turning around he returns up the brook to find Carter on the other side taking pictures where they found the body. He waves at him.

"I'll meet you at the tree line on this side."

He carries on, slower this time, unsure of what he's looking for but eying every broken weed, bent stalk of grass or any indentations. Following his own footsteps, he gets to where he discovered the grass distorted from a heavy object being dragged. As he had examined it before, he carries on to the large pine and glances in each direction. Standing where he was when the sergeant called out, he surveys the terrain in front of him - the bloody gloves. The upturned sod with the scent of fresh earth still strong, the empty cavity. The light is directly behind him, and the floor is dappled with light beams which undulate from the unsteady limbs above. It makes him feel as if he's not alone.

He watches where he steps. The dried leaves and puny twigs crunch under his feet. A mixture of hardwoods and softwoods of varying ages surround him on three sides. His back is to the field. The smell of dripping sap is strong near the spruce trees. Several tall ones shadow his right, young hardwoods on his left surrounding a long trunk of a dead tree, perhaps one of their ancestors. They spread out slightly to form an opening which faces him. Taller trees shroud the background, obscuring everything. He steps forward and crouches down with his butt on his heels to examine the hole. The edges at the bottom are sharp where the object settled in the ground. He can see the outline and three corners of something hard and rectangular.

He estimates the size to be about thirty inches by twenty-four or five. The bottom of the hole is a good two feet down. It's hard to tell how thick the object was. He stands and looks around slowly, eyes alert. There are footprints where the floor was disturbed. The gloves. Snapping one of the dead limbs on the bottom of a fir tree, he bends and pokes the stiff branch into the cuff of the glove, picking it up and rotating it in front of him. It's saturated with blood, especially on the palm with only the pinky untouched. The other glove is unstained. They would be too big for Kravchenko's medium hand. He returns them to roughly the same position.

When he stands, he notices that the sun has moved over the heavy canopy into the space left by the fallen tree. In the opening in front of him, the glint of a slick surface catches his eye. Walking around the hole, he pushes aside a fence of slender birch trees, infants no taller than himself. An umbrella of pines branches as thick as a man's leg creates a small empty clearing of needles and stray dying leaves. The ground is softer, and more footprints are evident. Ten steps ahead of him is the scene of a massacre.

10

10:37 am

Startled out of his stupor by the cracking of a branch behind him, Kravchenko sees Carter turning by the pine and calls out to him.

"Did you bring a flash?"

"Yes, I did, Sir, and lots of bulbs."

"Tread carefully around the hole and join me in here."

"Yes, Sir."

Carter stops near Kravchenko and gasps at the sight before him. Leaves and small branches on a cushion of dried needles are covered with blood, faded to a burgundy blush over an area as big as a bathtub. A few indents hold small pools of the gruesome gel. It looks like someone spilled a pail of it. Bare earth is exposed and the carpet of leaves is disturbed from a large object being handled; Kravchenko doesn't think it was a woodland creature.

A rope hangs from a sturdy branch directly above the mess. The coiled end hangs ten feet above the loop poised against the drab wood, reminding Kravchenko of a screaming mouth. The knotted circle is big enough for a pair of ankles. The other end is anchored to the trunk of a neighbouring maple. The dim light does nothing to hide the macabre scene. Kravchenko thinks out loud.

"This is where he butchered them."

"Pardon me, Sir?"

"We've found the spot where he cut them up, Carter. A ghastly scene."

"Could've been a deer, too, Sir. I've heard of poachers round about."

"I don't think so. I don't see any of the remains usually left behind by hunters, the insides, hoofs, their hides sometimes, antlers maybe. Whatever was done here, the culprit got rid of everything. Give me a moment."

He gets as close to the scene as he can, treading around the other footprints. He crouches and studies the terrain. Carter watches him and sees the concentration in the scrunched brows and tight lips. He's committed to doing what he can to help, even without having to be ordered.

Kravchenko looks beyond the blood stain. Closer to the trunk the ground is marked up where he thinks the killer struggled with the bodies. Remembering the cadaver at the hangar, he guessed a weight at about a hundred and eighty, heavy enough. With inadequate sunlight to see clearly, he removes a flashlight from a side pocket of his uniform trousers and moves the beam over the ground. The bloody earth is even more gruesome in the spotlight. There is nothing else to see.

He stands and casts the light around the perimeter of the small area and sees no other trees or openings, nothing else disturbed except for the way he came in. Directly across from him is a greyish trunk of a tree, thick and rotting. It died a decade ago, but the core is still strong, resisting its contest with gravity but it won't be long. It's surrounded by dried limbs which have already given up. Sweeping back over them, he sees a glint of reflected light.

"There's something there. Wait here Carter. Don't touch anything."

Kravchenko returns the light to his pocket and maneuvers through a cluster of fir trees, their hooped skirts overlapping each other. Ducking under branches of taller ones, he stops at the back where he saw the flash of light. A fishing rod. Beside it is a woven basket with a worn leather strap, turned upside down with its contents spilled on the ground.

Kravchenko has to move a couple of branches to get closer. He bends to inspect them, remembering to leave everything untouched in case the police have to be involved. Deciding there is nothing else to see, he stands and is about to turn back when something else a few steps deeper in the woods causes him to stop.

A stream of sunlight filters down through the canopy, lighting up the background to expose a group of tall maples surrounded by offspring of all sizes, their leaves a hundred shades of orange. A soft wind rattles the treetops, causing the leaves to whisper in the stillness. A streak of unnatural blue is hanging from a young tree. Kravchenko pushes aside the saplings and sees the sleeve of a shirt caught on a branch. Moving the obstruction, he discovers more clothing. He wants to collect them and remembers his earlier instructions to himself to leave things alone. He stands and rubs his chin, doffs his hat to scratch an imaginary itch. He thinks back to Group Captain Clark's remark.

"You investigate on the base with my authority. On civilian grounds, you might want to be... discrete."

He got the message: I'm behind you but I won't take the blame.

Right now, he's on land owned by the Department of Defense and technically still on base. They're vital clues. He grabs the shirt, and grimaces at the bloodied top, the dark trousers, the armless undershirt, boxer shorts and one sock. Swishing the branches about, he finds the other close by. From what he can see, the owner is not a big person, probably a small man or a woman. Placing the clothing in a bundle wrapped with the trousers, he trots back to join Carter.

"What ya got there, Sir?"

"Somebody's apparel. We'll have to check it out once we get it back to the base. Here's what I want you to do. Get several shots from all four sides. If you see anything odd or more footsteps, tell me ASAP. I'm going to set this down where we cross the brook and take a walk farther down the road coming into the field. When you're done here, come and meet me."

"The rope too, Sir?"

Kravchenko tilts his face to study the rope, the loop swinging in the breeze as if mocking them.

"Yes, Carter, the rope too."

11

Kravchenko drops his package and carries on to the road, stirring the dead grass. Seed pods scatter and drift in the airstream. He wipes the tiny burrs off the legs of his trousers and stares down the road along the field, taking in the surroundings. The day is warming, and he removes his hat to wipe the perspiration from his brow. On the left are trees and a crisscross fence of cedar poles with their bases trimmed with dried foliage. The mountain top of sawdust is visible beyond, the parked bike a hundred feet away. The road is straight with a slight bend where it enters the forest after the fields. It could not really be called a road, more like two tracks curved in the grass. Some spots are larger where water pools when it rains. The field is divided into sections growing in abandon all over. He's mesmerized for a moment when he watches the wind play havoc with the tall fronds and their feathery tops. They move in concert, as if practiced and follow the zephyr's silly mood.

"No time for daydreaming, Stefan."

He walks glancing around in the track to his right while checking the track opposite. Only bike tracks are obvious here. It takes him almost fifteen minutes to reach a couple of hundred feet from the tree line where the road enters and turns to the left to join Highway 134, which runs through Scoudouc. Footprints. One set but two directions. He is standing where the boot marks twist in the soil to go back in the opposite direction. He stoops to examine a clear print. Maybe a man's size eight.

He follows it to where another set joins it. Several feet behind the two pairs are tire marks. The disturbing feature of the two sets of footprints is they look like the pair were struggling, not standing still. He walks beyond the tire prints and there is only the one set of prints coming in, none going back out. He doesn't like what this tells him. Either the first person left in the car or...he shudders when he thinks of the other possibility.

He follows the footprints to the edge of the forest. Some are obliterated from the tires, but he can see they are the same. With nothing else of note he walks back to where the car stopped. Studying the ground more closely, he can see where the car reversed into the field and left again. When he surveys the terrain around him, an oddity draws his attention. Where the grass is waving in the wind, there is an area near the tree line without movement in the swath of rippling flower tops. He decides to check it out.

The fields are probably close to five or six hundred feet long and he wades through the dead grass until he comes to the spot where nothing was moving. It becomes clear why. It's a mound of earth where something... or someone, has been buried.

"Damn."

He sees Carter approaching him and yells out.

"Leave the camera by the side of the road and go get a shovel."

"Yes, Sir."

While waiting Kravchenko sees footprints he missed. They're ten feet from where he walked in. Two sets. Circling the mound, he finds one set walking along the edge of the forest toward the brook. It's more beaten down. If he discovers what he thinks will be in the hole, this is where the killer travelled back and forth to the spot where he, or she, dug up whatever was in the hole he first discovered, and where they dismembered the body. He follows it for a ways until Carter returns with a shovel. He returns to the disturbed earth and takes the shovel to start digging in the center. He only has to dig down eight or nine inches when the shovel hits a soft but unyielding spot. Dropping the shovel, he bends to scoop the dirt away to expose putrefying skin. A human. The stench of decaying flesh knocks him back as if he's been slapped.

"What a mess, and the stink."

He stands and looks at Carter who is standing on the other side of the grave pinching his nose.

"I expect it will be headless and I now see where the clothing might've come from. I don't understand why this corpse is naked. What's going on?"

"I don't know, Sir."

"I don't know either, Carter, but that's why we're here, isn't it?"

"Yes, Sir."

"I've seen enough. Cover the body so the bugs won't get at it for now, Carter, but before you do, take a few photos of what we see now. I'll have Sergeant Booth get a detail out here later with respirators and gloves to retrieve the body."

"Yes, Sir. What do I do after that?"

"Go get the photos developed and swear the person to secrecy using the Group Captain's authority. Go have lunch if you can stomach anything after this. I'll meet you and Sergeant Booth back at the hangar at sixteen hundred hours. Pass the message on to the sergeant if I don't run into him. The old dry-cleaning stub you found makes me curious. I think a quick trip into Moncton to check it out might be worth my time. It's really the only lead I have until we hear back from Sergeant Booth's inquiries."

12

At the same time Kravchenko is staring at the road into the fields, it is early evening in Berlin. Late in the workday. *Oberstleutnant* Dieter Schmitz of the *Abwehr* is worried. He paces back and forth in the small office he occupies at 8 *Prinz Albrecht* Street. A manila file lies yawning on the polished desktop. A clip holds a dozen copies of notes and forms. It's not very old. A photo. A brief, detailed account of who the man is. His alias. Placement. Date of dispatch. Rating of reliability, loyalty, and capability.

Stopping to lean over the papers, he scans it for the tenth time, barely giving the longer sections more thought. His superior's colleagues disregard the Scoudouc Air Force Base rumours and argue that the informant and the information is unreliable, the location illogical. They concentrate on the port of Halifax and Saint John. Schmitz's superior, *Oberst* Meyer felt otherwise and initiated his own undercover work.

He needs this to work but Schmitz questions a man of this age.

Manfred Becker.

Age: 53

DOB: 01/20/1888.

Father: Sigmund, killed in line of duty, 1916. Mother: Gertrude Baumann, deceased. No siblings.

Injured in 1918. A visible limp remains.

Alias: Samuel Thomas (Tommy) Wright

Code Name: Iron Spear

Placement: Moncton, New Brunswick, Canada. Secondary: Scoudouc, New Brunswick, Canada.

Date of Dispatch: March 1938.

Profession: Recent: Carpenter. Former: Butcher.

◘

Schmitz smirks at the last line. Sending a butcher for sabotage he can understand. Perhaps it was a wise move from Herr Himmler when he ordered infiltration of all allied countries while international travel was still unrestricted. In Canada's case, because of its close ties to Great Britain, people were placed in all provinces. The forward thinking of the Nazi regime has people in every corner.

His concentration is broken by a sharp rap on his office door.

"Enter."

Stabshauptmann Otto Müller steps into the office with boots clicking. Standing at attention in front of the large desk, he raises his right hand in the Nazi salute.

"Heil Hitler!"

Schmitz makes a half-hearted response.

"Heil Hitler."

The *Stabshauptmann* doesn't like the pomposity of the man.

"Anymore word from Iron Spear?"

"Nein, *Oberstleutnant.* Only the report you have before you. He has been activated upon your orders. There has been no confirmation of any new devices. I am wondering if this is subterfuge by our enemies. To mislead us?"

"You give them more credit than is due, Müller. Our sources in London have confirmed a shipment left two weeks ago under strict secrecy. It can only be what we expect it is. Is the submarine in place?"

"Jawohl, *Oberstleutnant.*"

Schmitz finally looks up to Müller. He notices the arrogance in the young man's mien. Time to take him down a notch.

"I expect action on this immediately Müller. Have a favorable report to me by this time tomorrow and if I'm not happy with what I am hearing, you may find yourself sequestered to the *Wehrmacht* and in the front lines. Do I make myself clear?"

Müller stares at the wall above his superior's head and snaps his boot.

"Very clear, *Oberstleutnant.*"

"Dismissed."

"Heil Hitler"

"Heil Hitler."

◻

Schmitz almost falls into his chair and drops the aggressive stare. His nerves are on edge. Beads of sweat appear on his upper lip and across his brow. His hand shakes when he dabs his forehead with a handkerchief. He received the same order from his immediate superior, *Oberst* Meyer. With the same punishment for failure. He looks up at the framed photo of the *Fuhrer.* As much as he idolizes the man, he fears being in the line of fire.

13

1:02 pm

Kravchenko decides to return to the hangar by following the footprints along the forest to search for anything amiss. With the sun behind him almost to the pine tree where he discovered the digging, he glimpses a slivery glint in one of the footprints. Actually several prints are bunched together, as if the walker turned around, looking in all directions or couldn't decide what to do. He stoops to dig in the trodden stalks and finds what looks like a keyring, more of a key ID, a round tag, with a metal rim. On one side of the white cardboard is a pound sign and a hastily scrawled number, #13. It's autographed by a smudged fingerprint on both sides. He's seen these before at repair shops. It's something else to go on, a new scent to follow. He loves his work.

Finding nothing else, he follows the brook once more, crosses over and heads back to the base. He's glad Carter showed him the shallow spot to cross. His boots have so much mink oil on them they repel most of the water, but his feet are still a bit damp and spongy from some water spilling into them earlier.

He leaves without running into either Booth or the GC and arrives in Moncton at 2:11. He hasn't eaten since breakfast and he's hungry. It takes more than dead bodies for him to lose his appetite. He recalls one of his buddies at the Saint John base telling him to try Hynes Restaurant on Mountain Road. The fish and chips are second to none according to him. He wants to sit and make notes of what he's discovered so far and start a list of tasks. The next step will be to go to the drycleaners which he expects to be a dead end. He's done enough snooping to know to follow up everything, even the mundane or those which don't seem to make sense. He's not familiar with the city and asks his waitress where he might find Sunrise Drycleaners.

She looks down at him with the bluest eyes he's ever seen and what he regards as a flirting look. She likes his wavy hair and luscious looking lips. Looks good in his uniform.

"Not from around here, are you, love? Well, the drycleaner is off Shediac Road. When you go out front, turn left and... uhm, let's see... turn left again five streets down, Botsford, runs right into Shediac Road. Can't miss the cleaners, big red sign on top. Will you be having anything else?"

He smiles at the waitress. She's a pleasant woman. He rubs his tummy.

"Oh goodness no. I'm full enough. The fries are excellent and so was the fish."

"Glad you enjoyed it, love. I'll get your bill."

With a weakness for a pretty smile, he leaves her a considerable tip. Noticing she had no wedding band or engagement ring, he thinks he might come back and ask her out when he wraps this up. But not today.

He finds the cleaners easy enough and parks his car. He likes this city. He's been to #5 Supply Depot before, which is still being developed in the northern part of the city. There are all newer homes along this street, some of them look expensive. With the trees aglow in their fall colors and a warm day, he regrets not being able to look around more. He sighs. Another day maybe. Concentrate on your job he thinks.

When he goes inside, he sees a middle-aged woman behind a long counter leafing through pages on a clipboard. She looks like she's in bad mood. No smile, no pleasantries, just a sour face and informal greeting.

"Help ya?"

He doesn't bother replying, just slides the unfolded stub across the counter.

She checks the name and looks up at him.

"I remember this. It's been here a while and I called to remind you yesterday, but the number wasn't in service."

Kravchenko keeps a poker face. The news is good.

"My boss asked me to pick it up. I think he said his wife dropped it off. You remember her?"

"Nope. This is Carmalita's handwriting. I was probably out back. This is not my usual job. Hang on and I'll get it for ya."

"Thank you."

She goes through an open door behind here where he can see a carousel with clothes shrouded in plastic hanging from it. He watches her press a button and the clothes move along like ghosts until it clicks in a spot familiar to her, likely alphabetical. She scans through a few pieces until she finds what she's looking for and removes a crisp uniform from the rack. Returning to the front, she hangs it on a hook on the side wall near the counter, rips of a tag stapled to the plastic and goes to the cash register.

"That'll be seventy-eight cents, please."

He doles out eighty cents in change. She returns two pennies and a cash register receipt and passes him the uniform.

"Thank you for your business, sir."

Still no smile but at least she thanked him before returning to the clipboard. He examines the uniform while walking back to the car. It has the blue band around the cuff signifying the uniform is for an air commodore, one of the big brass, like a one-star general in the army. He's even more confused. If an air commodore was missing, it would be big news. And he's heard nothing of the sort. There are no air commodores in New Brunswick as far as he knows. The nearest one is at RCAF Station Debert in Nova Scotia. He better get the sergeant to check on this too.

Folding it in half, he places it on the back seat and sits at the driver's wheel fingering the paper disc he found earlier. Good time as any to ask around. He thinks of where he would go if he was undercover.

If a repair shop is giving out tags they must be busy, or it could be part of an inventory. Looking at his watch, an Omega issued by the Air Force, he sees that it's almost two-thirty. He told the others to meet him at the hangar at 16:00. It only takes him a half hour or less to get back, so he'll go check some repair shops and car dealers. When he drives off his mind is on the deadline. He has until Friday morning to solve this or pass it on to the police. It will be the GC's decision, not his.

14

3:10 pm

Kravchenko has visited six service stations, three car dealers and two body shops with no luck in identifying the tag. Checking the time, he decides to try one more. At the end of St. George Street where it curves northward toward Mountain Road in front of the Canadian National Railway repair shops is a dealer of used cars and repair station. Above the bay doors is a white plastic sign with bold blue letters that says *Bud's New & Used*. The office is located in a smaller building to the left in front of a selection of assorted autos. A huge picture window opens to the parking lot through which Kravchenko can see an overweight man at a desk smoking a cigar. Wisps of smoke circle his smooth dome with close cut hair on the sides over big ears.

Kravchenko parks his car in an empty slot near the smaller building. The man sits up, attentive, thinking of a possible sale. All smiles, he meets Kravchenko at the door. Red braces, over a checkered shirt hold up a pair of woolen slacks with polished knees The man has the cigar stuck in his mouth and an eye closed against the curls of smoke. One hand is shoved in a pocket and the other is held out to be shaken.

"Hello there, Soldier. Looking for a good used car?"

The words are strung together with a clacking sound. Kravchenko notices the false teeth which are a size too big, dropping on certain letters and pushed back up with the tongue.

"Not today, I'm afraid, Sir. My name is Stefan. I'm working with the boys out in Scoudouc and I have something you might be able to help me with."

The man has a disappointed look and drops the hand. The smile is replaced with a frown.

"What might that be?"

Kravchenko holds out the tag.

"Have you seen this before?"

"Yeah, it looks familiar."

He takes it from Kravchenko and studies it a moment.

"Name's Bud, by the way."

Kravchenko eyes the sign and assumes he's talking to the owner.

"Think that might be from here, Bud?"

"Yep. That's my handwriting, as sloppy as it is. My helper is always complaining I should practice my numbers. He gets them mixed up sometimes."

He starts to pocket the tag when Kravchenko waves at him.

"I need to keep that please, Sir, if you don't mind. What can you tell me about it?"

Bud shrugs and passes the tag back to him.

"It's an inventory tag. I have them on all the keys for the cars that are for sale."

"Would you know which vehicle it comes from and when it was sold?"

"Let me see it again."

He tales a quick glance.

"Hmmm, number 13. Give me a minute and I'll check."

Bud waddles back through the open office door. Kravchenko follows and waits at the doorstep. He watches the man leaf through a logbook of some sort and pause after a few pages.

"Yep. A '35 Dodge. I remember now, I was glad to get rid of that one. The piston rings were going, starting to fart out some blue smoke when you revved it up."

Kravchenko gets a neck tightening rush when he discovers

something new.

"What can you tell me about the car, color, marks, or anything like that?"

Bud becomes a little suspicious and looks askance at the soldier.

"What do you need information like that for?"

Kravchenko heeds the GC's warning of secrecy.

"On of our flyer boys went AWOL. Found this on his nightstand and thought it might be worth looking up."

"It was nothing eye catching, grey body, black fenders and running boards. Kinda plain. Buffed up it didn't look too bad. The ram sitting proudly in front. Always was my favorite hood ornament, kept it shiny myself. There's a small dent on the passenger's back fender."

"Remember the man that bought it?"

"Not well. My part timer, Moe Leblanc, sold it. I was here that morning getting some transfers looked after and other paper shenanigans. I get behind on that stuff. I have a vague recall. It's been a while...let me see."

Bud checks the logbook, runs his finger across the name over the line as if touching it will make his memory sharper.

"Nah, can't really remember a face. It was last winter. Date is February 14th. Hah, look at that. Maybe a Valentine's present, do you think?"

With a soundless laugh at his own joke, his two chins dance. Then the smile does an about face. He looks up to Kravchenko in the doorway.

"I remember one thing about the bugger now. It was those damn eyes. Kinda spooked me. He was a grinin' all the time but not the eyes. Yeah, I was glad when he left. But I can't remember the face or anymore about him. Sorry."

Kravchenko's nods along, eager to know more.

"Is Moe around?"

"Nope, you boys sent him overseas. Gone a couple of months now. He's somewhere in England learning how to kill the damn Krauts. Pardon me language."

Kravchenko points to the register.

"Did you get a name?"

Another glance, the finger trailing the entry.

"Leading Aircraftsman Elmer Coleman."

15

The gigantic hangars at the Scoudouc Base take up the front section by the landing strip. A road runs parallel to the back of the buildings, out the gate, through the fields beyond, over the brook and out to Highway 134. Rows of buildings, barracks, supply warehouses and stores, maintenance facilities, repair shops, infirmary, administration buildings, mess hall and the motor pool make up the opposite side. The base has hundreds of employees, both military and civilian. Non-military people make up forty percent of the base population, the majority working from eight until five-thirty seven days a week. The rest work on night shifts, at the hospital, the heating plant, kitchen, laundry, maintenance, and stores. The military handle the guard duty.

One of the administration buildings is strictly off limits. A two-man unit is posted in front twenty-four hours a day in three shifts. It's not uncommon to see guards posted around the base. In fact, it is imperative for security. Infiltrators and thieves are possible threats. Non-descript in every way, this building is painted in flat grey paint over plain wooden clapboard walls. A covered stoop stands out in front with three wide steps. A dim light shines in the porch over a wooden door barring entry. There are no windows. A ten-foot lawn stretches in front, split by a brick walkway wide enough for three people abreast. Several antennae stick up from the roof, shiny chrome and straight like tines of a fork. The only charming aspect of the building is the flower boxes in front with asters blooming in purple glory.

In front by the street is a six-by-six hut with an open doorway and glass on the upper half all the way around except for corners. Its main use is for rain protection. Of the two guards posted when Kravchenko arrives, one is huddled inside the hut checking IDs for anyone trying to gain admittance. It's a short list and he ticks off the box beside Kravchenko's name. The other guard is navigating the area around the building. The night has a sharper, cooler edge with the temperature dropping and heavy cloud cover moving over the coast, making the evening somber.

Kravchenko has a lot on his mind when he meets up with Sergeant Booth, GC Clark and AC2 Carter, who are all gathered in a lab style room at the back of the building. Having passed through yet another guard posted inside the main entrance, he walks into the lab and finds four men gathered around an odd-looking device in the middle of the floor. The conversation stalls and they all look up at him when he enters the room. GC Clark waves him over.

"Dr. Sylvester Flewelling is explaining the function of the cavity magnetron to us, Kravchenko. Come join us."

He introduces Kravchenko to Dr. Flewelling and the scientist carries on.

"So, when the magnetron is exposed to a strong magnetic field, we can generate wavelengths in the microwave range, above infrared radiation and below radio waves in the electromagnetic spectrum, and..."

He continues for the next ten minutes explaining the functions and usefulness of the magnetron and why it is being tested in secret. Most of what he tells them is lost on the men. What interests them most is how beneficial the discovery is to direction finding and how it could help to win the war.

"When we receive a radio signal, as well as our comrades in Coverdale listening station, we can pinpoint its source with greater accuracy. If the signal source is unknown, it is evidence of a rogue radio transmitter or worse, a U-boat."

Kravchenko is paying close attention to what the man is explaining and a thought occurs to him.

"Is it operational now?"

"Yes, it is. All frequencies are being monitored at all times. The next room to us is manned twenty-four hours a day. The signal is verified and logged."

"Who is notified when a signal is detected?"

"Myself, of course, as well as Group Captain Clark. It is limited to the two of us at present."

Kravchenko looks to the Group Commander.

"May I be added to the list, Sir?"

GC Clark nods to both Kravchenko and Flewelling. Wrapping up his presentation, Flewelling is heading home, escorted out by GC Clark. The other three men move to an adjacent office where they clear a large center table and pull up chairs to discuss what they've found. They wait for Clark to return and he joins them at the head of the table. He looks to Kravchenko.

"What do we have so far, Kravchenko?"

"Well, sir, we have two dead bodies, one, possibly two, headless. One head has been recovered. We have the uniform of a leading aircraftsman, and I am now in possession of an air commodore's uniform which I picked up at the cleaners in Moncton using the tag Carter found in the pocket of the LAC uniform. While searching the site where something was buried, I also found a key tag which I traced down to a garage in the city. It is for a 1935 Dodge of which I have a complete description. Both the dry-cleaning tag and the car purchaser belonged to Leading Aircraftsman Elmer Coleman. I would bet my bottom dollar it's a fake name but one to search for nonetheless. I also have a fishing rod and creel and a suit of clothing which I have yet to go through."

"No answers yet?"

"No, Sir. I sent Sergeant Booth on a search. What did you discover, Sergeant?"

Booth has a notebook out, a smaller one with the metal spiral along the top. He flips it open.

"I checked on all bases in New Brunswick as you suggested but finding no results, I took the liberty of going beyond and checked other Maritime bases and there are no missing uniforms of any rank. All personnel missing from bases have been accounted for... except two. Neither one is a LAC. AC1 Vernon MacKinnon of the RCAF Detachment Salisbury left for a family funeral in Prince Edward Island on October 4th. Funeral's today. He is due back day after tomorrow. The other is Corporal Lance Smythe of the Basic Training Center in New Glasgow in Nova Scotia. He was reported AWOL October first."

Kravchenko makes note of the two names in his own pad. GC Clark sits forward with hands clasped on the table, eyes guarded and worry on his brow.

"Did you follow up on Smythe?"

"Yes, Sir. Talked to a Lieutenant Marchand with the SP in New Glasgow. The family in Ontario, New Delhi to be specific, along the tobacco belt, have been notified and have no idea of his whereabouts."

Clark interrupts the Sergeant.

"Or are not telling."

"I suggested the same thing, Sir."

Kravchenko catches the subtle ass kissing by Booth. It doesn't matter; he's a good non-com. Clark sits up straighter.

"Lieutenant Marchand commented the family seemed genuinely surprised, Sir. I'd like to believe them."

Kravchenko is nodding his head.

"Do you have a description of Smythe?"

"Yes, sir. On his last physical, he weighed a shade under one hundred and fifty pounds and is approximately five feet eight inches tall. The only visible scar is a three-inch knife wound on the lower right forearm."

Kravchenko continues his note keeping and makes a check mark beside the name Smythe.

"That eliminates him from the first body. Did the detachment sent out to recover the second body, bring it in yet?"

"Yes, Sir. It is in the same hangar, on ice, Sir."

"We'll look at it later. What about MacKinnon?"

"The family do not have a phone but there is an emergency number of the local post office. I've left a message and then called the funeral parlour. The funeral was over and everyone involved had already left. The funeral director could not recall seeing Vernon MacKinnon himself. I have not received a reply yet, Sir."

"Physical details?"

"Five foot ten and a half, one hundred and eighty-five pounds. Only visible scar is over the left eye, approximately an inch long, from a childhood accident."

The airman's size fits well with the first body and has Kravchenko's interest.

"What part of PEI is he from?"

Booth has to refer back to his notes and flips several pages over.

"A small community called Augustus, east of Charlottetown."

"Ok. Good work, Booth. Get a hold of WO1 Bordage at the Charlottetown base. He's with the Service Police there. Ask him to send someone to check on MacKinnon and to please report back ASAP."

"Yes, Sir."

Clark checks his watch and directs his attention to Kravchenko.

"I have an appointment so I must leave you, Gentlemen. Keep me posted if anything new comes up."

Everyone rises from their seats and salutes the GC and he leaves. Kravchenko points to the folder Carter has before him.

"Let's have a look at the photos you took, Carter."

"Yes, Sir."

Carter pulls them out. They are all 5 X 7's and he puts them in order on the table. There are twenty-one. Kravchenko and Booth are standing behind Carter as he lays them out. Once he is done, he steps back so the three of them can scrutinize the black and whites.

Kravchenko pays close attention to the footprints where the body was found. There is a clear indentation of a boot heel in one of the photos. He speaks to Carter.

"Can you have whoever developed the photos make an enlargement of this one, closing in on the heel imprint to see if it can come out clearer."

"Yes, Sir."

After going through the rest of the photos, one of the images from the scene in the woods causes him to pause over it. Picking it up, he looks closer. The photo is of the hole and the dirt which was dug up. Carter took the picture facing the entrance. At the edge of the brown dirt is a half footprint, the heel dominant. He reaches for the other heel imprint and examines it quickly. They look the same but at different angles. He's not sure. He stares at the wall in front of him thinking of possibilities.

If they are the same, the killer would've pulled the body out of the water downstream, but why? Was he taking it somewhere else, using the water to transport it? Looking for motives is difficult enough but much worse when the victims are unknown. He needs to identify these corpses as soon as possible. Look for the car. People missing in the community. Look at the other body. Check the clothes he found. Widen the search for missing uniforms. He refocuses and passes the two photographs to Carter.

"Get the heel prints enlarged as best as they can be, Carter."

"Yes, Sir."

"Sergeant Booth, broaden your search. Check on missing people as far as you can reach. Go to each supply depot in the system, on and off bases. Tell them you are checking on behalf of the Group Captain Carter's orders and the Service Police. And again, follow up on MacKinnon and Elmer Coleman. Now I'm going to check the other corpse and I'll see you both here in the conference room at the hangar at oh-seven hundred tomorrow morning."

"Yes, Sir."

"Yes, Sir."

16

8:01 pm

Kravchenko enters the hangar, greeted by the two airmen on guard duty. They check his ID and the list, clearing him to go to the second room where the body is. Booth and Carter arranged for large tubs to be filled with ice from Maritime Ice - large blocks that melt slowly. It has reduced the smell considerably but the second body still stinks. The method of execution is the same, a knife under the ribs into the heart. Dirt from the grave is in the wrinkled skin. The only clue derived from viewing the body is confirmation that the head they found belongs to this torso. Nothing else makes sense. Kravchenko realizes he'll have to wait to hear back if MacKinnon is missing before making any assumptions.

He can't even guess why the corpse is naked, why it has been disrobed and the clothing discarded. Why were the heads removed? One still missing. The only thing Kravchenko picks up on is that the killer went to a lot of extra work. Why the uniform? Or could it be, and he frowns at the crazy idea, only to create confusion: gruesome dealings to draw attention away from something else happening... or about to happen?

After checking for any identifying marks, and finding nothing else, he goes to another room where the clothing is laid out. No wallet, no ID, nothing except pocket lint. The boots are common work boots. He checks the heels. On the left boot, there is an indent with a company logo in the center, partially worn. The boots are old and hard workers, the leather cracked and stiff and the edge of the heel rounded. The boots and clothing refuse to give him any more clues.

He's frustrated, thinking of the deadline GC Clark has given him. With another thirty-six hours and no hard clues to go on, he's not sure of his next move. He decides to call it a night, go to the barracks he's been assigned to and check his notes. When he is about to leave, he's interrupted by the inner guard who has been posted at the sawhorses.

"Warrant Officer Kravchenko, you are wanted at the lab, or rather the listening post as it's called. They say it's urgent, Sir."

Kravchenko thanks the guard and tells him to contact Sergeant Booth and leaves for the building he was earlier in. He notes the time on his watch. 10:22 PM.

17

Earlier

Iron Spear received a letter this morning, from his aunt in Pokemouche, a community in northern New Brunswick. It was hand delivered to his mailbox. No such person exists. He has no idea who sent it but it changes his plans. Under the lamp in his den over a scarred-up desk, he rereads the letter again.

> *My dearest nephew.*
> *I know you two were close and it breaks my heart to tell you. Your uncle Woody passed away. If you can make it, the funeral is on Monday at 10 in the morning at Riverside Baptist. I hope my letter finds you on time. I think there's a train out of Moncton and you should take it. Love you, honey.*
> *Aunt Dora*

He understands and reads the hidden meaning. Monday plus two, Wednesday at 10 PM, a message coming from *Unterseeboot* 498. That's today. And the biggest change was to steal the magnetron. He scoffs at the suggestion. He knows who it comes from : Klaus Schreiber, aka William Fitzsimmons, owner of the Pig & Hammer Pub in Toronto's east end, the most senior *Abwehr* agent in Canada. The man expects the impossible. He remembers his last contact, a woman pausing at the produce counter at the general store here in Scoudouc. Her hat was pulled low so he couldn't see her face. Grabbing a bag of apples from the selection in front of him, she brushed his hand, leaving instructions in a folded note. The gesture was simple and practiced. The page contained a drawing of what the object might look like and said to expect shipment by mid to late September and to get as many photos as possible. Not much to go on, and now he's expected to steal it.

◻

With only an hour of daylight left he takes his jacket and gloves, looks in the trunk of his 1935 blue and black Dodge to check on the case there, while trying to think if he forgot anything. He drives to the top of a peninsula and stops at Cap-de-Cocagne, forty acres of forest and shrub on the northern-most tip, shaped like the head of an arrow. A quarter mile of mixed woods stretches along a rocky coast of loose shale, uprooted trees, dense brush, short stretches of silky sand and an unfettered view to the Northumberland Strait. It is fifteen miles of deep and open waters to the nearest coast of Prince Edward Island. A dirt road circumnavigates the peninsula and loops in rhythm to the shore. It cuts through the base of the triangle. The wooded areas fade out to open fields and a few farms and cottages where the beach calls out with lapping waves and sunrises which can make you dizzy with their splendour.

The northern stretch of the wooded area also has a cottage nestled off the road reached by sixty feet of gravel driveway which curls through dense trees. Normally only used in the summer by the owner, Iron Spear rented it for the winter, exclaiming he is too old to be in the army and that he wants a quiet place, close to nature, away from the noise and activity of the city to write his novel. It's a simple dwelling, one level, twice as long as its width. Wood shingles with the white paint peeling on the edges cover the building. It has a main door, and one large window, now curtainless and dark. The door and window trim visible in the car's lights when he parks in the driveway, is dark grey. The front of the house

60

faces a yard as long as the drive in. To the right is an apple orchard of a dozen trees, with a smattering of yellowing leaves still clinging, too afraid to be on their own. A strip of lawn is uncut with hardly any green in it. The water is close enough so the headlights are reflected back in moving slivers.

He cuts the lights and stares out toward the water, waiting for his eyes to adjust to the darkness. The southeastern sky is dim, the new moon gives little light. Wandering clouds mask the stars and it's perfect for his mission. Getting out of the car, he goes to the trunk and removes a hard bodied case with a stiff handle. Ignoring the cottage, he tramples through the long grass toward a short cliff at the left of the open area near the shore. He opens the case and removes a small dish-like antenna and sets it up on the foldable tripod. The transmitter/receiver is bulky but much more portable than the older units. It has a built-in power source he made sure was working properly. He sets the antenna up, pointing toward the open water. Shielding his flashlight, he checks his watch. He has a half hour before he has to send his signal.

o

At precisely ten o'clock, he stands up, points his flashlight toward the water and makes quick flashes – three shorts. Soon a voice comes from his receiver. Raspy and guttural, it has the heavy hint of an order.

"Stand down. Extraction unsafe. Change to next day. Midnight. Out."

He knows the sender expects no response. He dismantles his equipment and tucks it all back in the heavy case, thinking of the consequences of the change. Previously planning on striking Friday night, he'll have to delay the action until Saturday, right before he has to make the rendezvous with the sub at midnight. He grins and feels energized by the change. There are few places to hide this close to the base. So he can get in, get out, get off base and meet the sub. He won't have to hide. He remembers to pick up the uniform.

18

Kravchenko enters the guarded building and goes to the listening post. Inside he's met by Sergeant Booth and Leading Aircraftsman, First Class, Jean Doucette. Doucette is a smallish man with a pencil moustache on his slim face, excitement in his eyes. Saluting the warrant officer, Doucette passes him a typewritten page.

Signal detected at O-twenty-two hundred and eleven hours. 10:11 PM. Source unknown. 46.47 degrees latitude, -64.724 degrees longitude.

Source unknown is underlined in red ink. Kravchenko is adrift when it comes to longitude and latitude.

"What do these coordinates tell you AFC Doucette?"

"I've narrowed it down and…, from what I can tell, it's in the Northumberland Strait. In the open water, Sir. Could be anywhere between Cap-de-Cocagne and Bouctouche."

Kravchenko's brows go up and he looks to Booth who has his shoulders hunched in a I-don't-know gesture. It becomes clearer in Kravchenko's mind.

"A boat or ship, Sergeant Booth. Inquire with Group Captain Clark to see what assets we have in this area, and maybe inform the Navy in Halifax to send any available ship to this location ASAP."

"Yes, Sir."

This confirms his earliest thought of something in the works. It has to be about the magnetron. If someone is attempting to steal it, he... and Kravchenko stops for a moment to consider another possibility... or she... will need an escape plan, and one by water makes the most sense. He will double check with the GC in the morning and suggest a further tightening of security. His mind is spinning with possibilities but he feels he has little to go on. He still needs to identify the bodies. He'll get Carter in mufti in the morning to scour the village for missing people and go over Booth's latest inquiries.

"Any more news on missing servicemen, Sergeant?

"Not at present, Sir, but I have people working on it, and promise to have the information no later than oh nine hundred tomorrow.

"Great. We'll all meet back here in the conference room at oh-seven thirty. Right now, I'm bushed and need to get some sleep."

19

Iron Spear sits in the parking lot of Sunrise Drycleaners in a 1935 blue and black Dodge. He's furious. His eyes are almost bugling out of his head, he's so angry. His cheeks are on fire. That *verdammt* serving woman and the stupid manager! He had to get angry at first when she refused to give him the items with no ID. He explained he forgot his wallet and needed the uniform but she still refused his request. He made her call the manager and after a tongue lashing, accusing them of being unpatriotic, the manager broke out in a sweat, rubbing his hands together. He sent the woman to find it.

And then she told him the clothes were picked up yesterday and she showed him the wrinkled tag amongst yesterday's receipts. He was blustering at first, unable to believe what she was saying. He told her to look again, to no avail. He berated them for giving his uniform away. The manager wiped his brow, offered him his money back. Realizing there was nothing else he could do; he told the manager to stick his refund in his *mastdarm*.

He curses himself for breaking a cardinal rule, never speak in your mother tongue. His anger is no excuse. And worse, the vilest thing imaginable, the mousy manager wore a name tag with the surname Borowitz, meaning he is probably a damn Jew. Calming down, he reverses his auto and returns to Scoudouc. He'll have to go to Plan B and to do that he needs to work the night shift. A call to Marc-Denis Daigle

64

will fix him up. He hates the four to twelve shift. If offered to exchange for one starting at eight in the morning, he'll jump at it.

Iron Spear needs to be ready to strike Saturday night.

20

A half hour earlier.

Kravchenko is sitting in the conference room going over his notes, wondering if he is in over his head. He thinks the police should be involved but he's a soldier first and he follows orders. Any repercussions will fall on the GC's desk. He's checking his list of things to do. On top of the page, in bold letters he wrote – TWO BODIES. He scratches his head and wonders why two bodies, why were they in this restricted area and who are they? One was obviously fishing or going fishing and Kravchenko guesses he may have disturbed whoever was digging the hole. But why two bodies?   While pondering the identities, he's disturbed by the GC entering the room. He stands at attention and salutes.

"Good morning, Sir."

"Good morning. I wanted to speak to you before the other men arrive."

"Yes, Sir?"

"What's this I hear about a possible boat or ship in our waters, nearby?"

"With the unknown radio signal, it is best to cover all possibilities. It may have originated from an enemy ship or seagoing vessel."

"I find it hard to believe a German ship could be in the waters so near. How could they evade the defenses set up along our coastal areas? The Navy have it covered from Newfoundland to the Bay of Fundy."

Kravchenko can't understand the GC's reluctance and wonders what the man is thinking.

"With all due respect, Sir, it's a very large area and while I don't know much about boats or ships, it's a distinct possibility. The unidentified signal, according to AFC Doucette, originated somewhere in the Northumberland Strait and I thought it best to have the Navy check and commandeer any suspicious watercraft."

"That is all very well, Kravchenko. But before I put the Navy on alert and get more people involved, back me up with some proof. Report to me by seventeen hundred hours and have something to back up your suspicions. I'll decide then. Now I must be off. Carry on."

"Excuse me, Sir, but shouldn't we have more security around the magnetron?"

"I believe what we have in place is adequate. No one will get past the men stationed at the guardhouse and inside."

Yes, Sir."

Kravchenko is confused, especially considering the GC's insistence on having this wrapped up by Friday. Every lead should be followed up. He decides that regardless of the GC's instructions, he needs to get out on the water and find out for himself. He'll speak to Booth and Carter when they arrive. He only has to wait another few minutes when both men enter the room. After bidding each other good morning, they sit at the large table.

"Let's hear from you first, Sergeant Booth. What do we have in the way of missing aircraftsmen or military personnel?"

Booth was up late following any leads on the west coast as they are four hours behind.

"MacKinnon has been located so we can scratch him off the list. There are no other missing service men that cannot be accounted for. That's a dead end. I've had no luck with Coleman either but I have not heard back from all my sources yet. I did, however, discover missing uniforms at Air Force Base Winnipeg. LAC Petosky reported two missing uniforms. They've never been recovered. I tried to get more information from him but was told the missing uniforms are part of an ongoing investigation and he was not authorized to divulge any more information."

Kravchenko is thrown off by uniforms missing from a base so far away. Without more info, it is difficult to ascertain if the ones they have are some of the missing ones, and how they ended up here. If they are related, this web is much broader than he anticipated.

"Good work, Sergeant. I'd like you to check the uniform we have to see if there are any identifying marks or... anything to suggest it might be from Petosky and if you do, please verify it. We can pass that info on to my counterpart on the base."

"Yes, Sir."

Turning to Carter, he holds his hand out for the envelope Carter brought with him. Opening it, he finds three enlargements of boot prints. The ones from the digging site and the site of the first body are not a match. The third one is from the road in where the footsteps stopped and turned around.

"Take these photos, Carter, and compare the two pair of boots we have. The first from the site where the first body was, and the ones I found in the woods. Let me know what you find."

"Yes, Sir."

"Okay, Gentleman. We need to identify these bodies. If not missing servicemen, they might be from the village or close by."

He points at Carter.

"I need you to change into street clothes and scour the village and nearby areas. Go to grocery stores or service stations, restaurants, places like that where folks gather. Be discrete and ask around about folks missing. I know you'll think of something. Also, keep an eye out for a 1935 grey Dodge with black running boards. There's a dent on the back fender on the right side."

"I'll borrow my mate's car and get at it right after I check the prints, Sir."

"Good. Sergeant, I'd like you to check with all the police stations within a two-hundred-mile radius and check for the same thing - missing persons. If there are any, details would be good, especially physical so we can save time if they differ from our corpses."

"I'll get on it right away, Sir"

"Excellent. Now, do either of you know where we can hire someone with a boat that knows the area around the Northumberland Strait?"

Carter has his head down and is scratching his chin. After a moment, he looks up with a grin.

"I know just the man. Aris Robichaud from Richibucto is a retired fisherman and still has his boat. Folks call him Skip, might be short for Skipper but I don't know. He dolled the boat all up and sometimes takes people out to fish or just for fun. If you check in the telephone directory, you should be able to reach him. He's probably free as most folks only go out on weekends and he's not as busy with the war going on."

"Is this someone I can trust with a little information?"

"Oh yeah. He's a veteran of the First World War and his son is in the Navy."

"I'll contact him. Anything else, Gentlemen?"

The others are shaking their heads and rising from the table when someone knocks on the door. Booth is the nearest and opens it. Outside is LAC Doucette. He passes a flimsy to Sergeant Booth.

"This telegram came for you, Sergeant. It's marked urgent."

Booth's brows shoot up when he reads it and wordlessly passes it to Kravchenko. The warrant officer's eyes are drawn to the body of the message.

Leading Aircraftsman Elmer Coleman was found dead 08/08/1941. Knife wound to the chest. Military and Civic Investigation ongoing.

Kravchenko looks at the originator. Warrant Officer 2 Blaine Collins. Canadian Air Force Base Winnipeg (South).

"This can't be a coincidence. Stolen uniforms, dead Air Force personnel, all from same base. Looks like stolen identity as well."

He checks his watch.

"Winnipeg is two hours behind us, so only oh-six hundred and ten there. I'll contact Collins later. Maybe he can shed some light on what's happening. But if their investigation is still ongoing, it might not be much. Let's meet back here at eighteen hundred hours. Carry on, Gentlemen."

21

Aris Robichaud, aka Skip, is a congenial soul, one of those people you take to immediately. His ever-present smile is smothered by a bushy white moustache which droops on the sides. He has the biggest potbelly Kravchenko has ever seen on such a short man. He's dressed in a white T-shirt over sturdy looking shoulders. Bright blue suspenders hold up clean but well-worn dungarees, the bottoms rolled up and faded in the knees and buttocks. Thin strands of whitish hair are trying their best to cover a tanned dome. His puffy cheeks glow with a sunburnt polish and his eyes speak of a man who is happy with his lot.

Kravchenko is standing by the gunwale of the boat as Skip motors from the wharf. The rushing wind makes him almost lose his hat. A quick grab keeps it from floating in the harbour. Looking around, Kravchenko is impressed at how neat and clean the boat is. It's a forty-footer with seats all around the open area, the cockpit roofed with its back open. Skip's standing in front of the helm as close as his belly allows. His green rubber boots are firmly planted for any sudden motion. The boat is glaring white with three red stripes along the waterline and she's named *Terese*.

Skip's following the line of buoys that lead through the dunes to open water. Kravchenko studies the sandbars which make a funnel out to the strait. A wooded island sits off to starboard only its northern tip visible. A warm breeze comes from the north and the hardwoods wave their autumn flags.

"What is that island over there, Skip?'

"That'd be Indian Island. It's a reserve for our native friends. There's plenty of smart fisherman from the island. Chief's name is Barlow, a good man. Once we get out past the dunes, we'll turn south and head toward Cap-de-Cocagne."

Skip opens the throttle once they are clear of the markers, steering the craft south.

"You sail these waters often?"

"Humph. Been sailing them since I was six, *avec mon père*. With me father. As far north as the Miramichi, south to Cape Tormentine and along the west side of PEI from West Point to Borden. Been fishing the strait since I was twelve. This boat belonged to my *père*. I had it fixed up good."

"Yes, it's a beautiful boat. You did a great job. Your dad would be proud."

Skip darts him a look from the wheelhouse and sticks up his chin.

"*Oui, oui*, he would."

Kravchenko likes the old man. He sees how happy the fellow is at the helm, his cheeks redder and his smile glued on.

"Have you seen any strange or unusual boats or ships lately?"

"Nothing out of the ordinary. Lots of pleasure craft over the summer but they're all put ashore now. Lobster season is still open in these waters and you'll see plenty as we get out farther. I'll be thinking about that while were sailing."

"How long until we get to Cap-de-Cocagne?"

"It's a couple of hours from here. The wind is at our back, the water's not making a fuss, so maybe a little better."

Kravchenko stands to the left of Skip where another seat of black leather with a slim back is bolted to the floor. It has a chrome step to hoist yourself up to bar stool height. His side of the dash has several gauges, a Majestic marine radio and in the center a compass, the glass glinting in the sun behind them. In front is a wide window. The festival of color is cut in half by the horizon, the deep blue of the water, almost cobalt. The sky is glorious, thinks Kravchenko, the color of sapphires. Gulls cross their path, shrieking for attention. The prow, as pleased as Skip's chin, cuts through the calm sea. He's glad for the good weather. Skip notices him watching the shore to the starboard side. He points to a cabinet door in front of Kravchenko.

"Look in the cabinet beside you and you'll find binoculars. Look around."

Pulling open the door, a hefty pair of magnified eyes is nestled in a woven basket attached to the inside of the cupboard. Turning them about in his hands he recognizes them as Zeiss, the same as what the Air Force use.

"These are nice, Skip."

"Well, if ya got to be looking for something, it's best to have the best. Wife gave me those a couple of years ago for my seventy-fifth birthday. Busted my old ones a week before."

Kravchenko moves to the starboard gunnel which comes up to his waist. Leaning against it he steadies the binoculars to scan the coast. He sees a lot of beach and sandy locations with straw grass as tall as a man waving from the shoulders. Wooded stretches, cliffs and rocky shores, sand mounds, crooked inlets and dead trees and an odd house or cottage repeat the pattern all the way to the next wharf. Skip answers the question in his mind.

"That's Cap-Lumiere, small fishing village. Wife is from there. Lots of pretty girls around here... uhm, what do I call you by the way? Do I gotta call you by your rank?"

Kravchenko grins at the man's serious look, shakes his head.

"No, no. Call me Stefan or Steven. I'll answer to either. In all your travels on the water, Skip, are there many places a boat could hide and not be seen from land or water?"

Skip glances at him with a questioning look and a lopsided smile.

"*Ah oui*, lots of places, me lad. There are rivers, big and small. Coves and creeks, all kind of places. Listen..., uhm Steve, it's likely not my business and I know this ain't no for-fun ride. It might be better you tell me what you're looking for so's I can help. You know any secret is good with me. I was in a war; I know how terrible it can be. You can trust me."

Kravchenko likes the look, both innocent and hurt, the old man gave him.

"I already knew that Skip. There's folks who vouched for you."

Skip's chest inflates, he stands up straighter, still looking to water. He acknowledges Kravchenko's with an *I-told-you-so* nod.

"I held back information because my orders are to keep as much hush hush as possible but I can override that order if I deem it necessary and yes, better for you to know. We, the Air Force, have two bodies on our premises at the Scoudouc base."

Skips brows shoot up, startled by the news.

"Dead, I expect."

"Yes."

"How come there's no police. Shouldn't they know what's going on?"

"Both bodies were found on Department of National Defense's property abutting the base. We are trying not to raise a panic and to keep it enclosed because one of the bodies was dressed in an Air Force uniform. My commanding officer has given me orders to find out what is going on. I have until tomorrow morning. But the most important thing and why we are here, we discovered an unknown radio signal. It was thought to be in these waters at a given latitude and longitude. From Cap-de-Cocagne to Bouctouche. I'm hoping to find its source. Had to be a boat or ... a ship."

Skip is digesting the information and concentrating with a stern look. Controlling the boat is mechanical and his mind searches the shores he's seen a thousand times. Kravchenko looks up at the ocean-going vessels, two of them, sitting at anchor about a mile offshore, perched on the horizon. He knows the Navy has an Isles class armed trawler cruising major New Brunswick ports in the southeast, the

HMCS *Baffin*, if he remembers clearly. They'll have checked them out. As far as he can tell from the radioman at the base, the signal was located in an unlikely position.

Skip concentrates on his navigating, staying as close to shore as safety allows. Kravchenko looks for anything odd, not knowing what he should be searching for. Antennae for sure and boats in wrong or suspicious places. He is watching the coastline when he spies a land mass stretching to their front. He has to holler over the humming of the diesel engine.

"What's the stretch of land to the southwest?"

"They call it the Bouctouche Dunes, nothing fancy but almost four miles long. If you want to enter Bouctouche River or see the village we have to go around."

"Yes, I think we should. We have enough time?"

"Yep."

"They have a wharf?"

"Yes, Sir. A busy one too. If you look to the port side, you can see a couple of ships at anchor. There must be one tied up in Bouctouche now, loading logs most likely or lumber. Ships come here often since the war started. I believe once they're full they bunch up in Halifax and join a convoy. It's scary out there with them damn U-boats."

Talking about U-boats has Kravchenko thinking of the possibility of one in these waters. It seems unlikely but with a war going on anything is possible.

Bouctouche offers nothing. It is a small town with plenty of activity on the waterfront. A scarred and weary seafarer, paint peeling at the bow, longer than the wharf with working davits, is hauling up bundles of logs with thick leather straps. On the wharf trucks are backed under the cranes waiting or being unloaded. With so many young men at war, many workers are more than middle aged and probably glad for the work.

They cruise at low idle under a bridge of heavy wooden beams and steel girders to sail out into a basin a half a mile across and half as much in front of them to the west. The body of water tapers to a point where it slims down to a narrow river. Skip takes them close to shore and does a circuit of the basin. Kravchenko studies the terrain, mostly short cliffs, or sand bars, lots of alders and trees. Once in a while he lifts the binoculars hanging around his neck to look closer. Several cottages, fields on the south side. Nothing.

"Let's head back out, Skip. Thanks."

Kravchenko is caught unaware when Skip opens the throttle. The sudden surge of the powerful engine tosses him backward toward the stern and he lands on the deck, his bum taking all the weight. One hand clutches the binoculars to his chest. Skip's laughing hard enough to make his gut wiggle.

"Hang on buddy. Don't want you falling off. Saving you is extra."

Kravchenko rises with a sour face, rubbing his left buttock. He can't decide whether to be angry or to start laughing. He bets the old bugger has done it before.

"That wasn't nice."

"Whatever are you talking about, Steve?"

The look of indignation is practiced, close to perfect. Kravchenko sees through it.

"Giving it the gas. Didn't warn me."

"My dear man, I'm only operating my boat in the manner I was hired to. Time is of the essence. Perhaps you'd like to sit in the back. In the ladies' section."

The boat takes a sudden tick to port when Skip's guffaws disturb his belly, which disturbs the helm. He corrects it instinctively. Kravchenko is holding on to the gunnel and frowning. He laughs at the old man's shenanigans. The ladies' section, indeed.

When the boat evens out, he props himself against the starboard gunnel and continues to scan the shoreline. A road follows the coast, he can see autos going close to shore. There are more homes here. Farms and harvested fields. Stretches of sandy shores. They bypass two wharfs. Kravchenko asks Skip to go closer so he can view the boats docked at each. One in St. Thomas and the other in Cormierville. Nothing odd. They cruise for another ten minutes and Skip points out the community of Cocagne and the basin. The bay around Cocagne is wide and an island sits offshore. Kravchenko moves back to stare out the window in the cabin beside Skip.

"That island worth looking at?"

"There's nothing there but trees and more trees, maybe a deer or two that walked over on the ice and got stranded. Once there was a house on the island but a long time ago it was moved across the ice by a team of horses. There is only a vacant hole there now. Nowhere to hide a boat."

"Ok. Is Cap-de-Cocagne far?"

"Nope, you can see the tip from here if you look to port. Should I sail close?"

"Please. And take me around the peninsula. If we find nothing then turn your boat north."

Skip motors the boat closer to Cocagne and a short way up toward the river before turning toward Cap-de-Cocagne. He rounds the tip. Kravchenko watches the shore through the binoculars. He sees only the odd house and smaller buildings like cottages. More sand, more cliffs. Nothing to hint of anything out of place. Disappointed, he asks Skip to take him back. When they return around the head of the peninsula of Cap-de-Cocagne, Kravchenko sees a reflection of light from the shore. He raises the binoculars and sees four people with telescopes on tripods on the farthest edge of the sandy beach, three men and a woman. The telescopes are pointed out into the bay and one of the males is writing in a notebook. He yells out.

"Hold on, Skip. Head back toward those folks on the beach."

Skip turns and sees the group.

"I can only get about fifty feet from the shore. It's too shallow there at the tip."

"That's fine, Skip." Skip motors in slowly until he feels a nudge from the front of the boat when it hits bottom. He puts it in neutral and eyes Kravchenko with raised brows.

"Keep it close, Skip."

Kravchenko undoes his boots and socks, rolls up his pantlegs to over the knees and slides over the side of the boat. Water goes over his rolled-up threads.

"Damn. Was hoping to stay dry," he cursed. "Oh well, all in the line of duty."

"You talking to me, Steve?"

"No, just to myself. Hang tight for a minute."

Kravchenko wades to shore, cringing at how cold the water is. The foursome stop their activities and watch him come toward them. He introduces himself to the lady who is in the forefront and guesses she is about twenty years older than the young men. She tells him her name is Brenda. She has a short haircut full of curls and happy eyes.

"Have you and your... friends been here long, Brenda."

"All afternoon actually. Why do you ask?"

"I was wondering what you're looking for, and if any of you saw any strange watercraft or anything unusual in the bay?"

She points to the three adolescents, Kravchenko guessing them to be close to sixteen.

"These are my students. I am with the Institute St. Joseph and we are watching for seals that journey here sometimes in the fall. And I haven't seen anything odd. Have you, boys?"

Three heads shake their heads in unison until the tallest one steps forward. He sticks out his hand and Kravchenko shakes it.

"Name's Ben. I didn't see anything strange today but I was up on the bluff..."

He turns and points to a finger of land which sticks out from the wooded tip. It's all rock and long grass.

"... looking at the stars last night and the lights across the bay when I saw a reflection from something beyond in the open water. It only lasted a second and it was difficult to see with only starlight. It kind of struck me as odd but I forgot about it until you asked if we saw anything strange."

"What time was it? Do you remember?"

"Not the exact time but it was shortly after ten."

"Nothing else?"

"No."

"Thank you then. Enjoy your day."

Kravchenko wades back out to the boat, mumbling to himself, wondering what the boy saw. The timing agrees with AFC Doucette's report on the signal. His mind goes to the only possibility, a menace that gives him a worse chill than the cold water he's in. A submarine! He has to warn the GC. Crawling back in the boat, he tells Skip he's ready to go but Skip makes a suggestion.

"I can do that but I've been thinking of possible hiding places for a boat. I know a spot where the rumrunners used to hide at one time during prohibition. We'll check it out."

22

9:22 am

Aircraftsman Carter, enjoying working undercover, is dressed in civilian clothes. He couldn't be happier helping the WO And Sergeant Booth. This is sure to get him to AFC 1 if he doesn't mess up. It's a sunny day and he's got the long sleeves of his plaid shirt rolled up to the elbows. His navy dungarees are almost new and tucked into the open top of his old work boots. He starts out in the town of Richibucto, follows the coast through Cap-Lumiere, on to Bouctouche, then Cocagne and bypasses Shediac because he's going back to the base at Scoudouc first. He needs to get another shirt. It's too hot for long sleeves and he has to dump the undershirt.

He's been mixing in, listening where he can, making small talk, at the wharves, service stations, the grocery stores, anywhere a group of people are hanging out. Most folks are talking about the war. The Germans keep gobbling up countries. Hitler is crazy. Young men going off to fight, some not coming back. Weather and politics. He's devised a reasonable and believable opening for his queries.

"Can you tell me if I'm on the right road to Moncton? I'm terrible with directions and don't want to get lost. I did one time and went missing for two days. Ever happen to you?"

About six out of ten people react to the last question first, saying, "Oh, yeah I've been lost before." A brief conversation. Carter is by nature a friendly man and people warm up to him. He maneuvers the chatter along and with a lower voice, confidentially, says, "I heard a young man is missing from around here. Is that so, or is it just a rumour?"

They usually look at him direct, eyes growing curious. All the replies are negative except one. In Cocagne a man at the restaurant, where he stopped for a coffee and made inquiries, said a woman was in looking for her brother this morning, fella named Pierre. She didn't seem too worried saying she's used to him wandering off. He went camping or something like that. The man doesn't know her but Carter gets a description of the woman and intends to follow up. It's a good lead.

He's frustrated by the time he gets to snoop through Scoudouc. It's almost noon and after he finishes changing his shirt for a cooler short-sleeved one, he's hungry. He gases up at the service station, asks around and then stops at the grocery store, buys an egg salad sandwich from one of the new coolers and a cola. He glares at the clerk when she tells him pop has gone up to eight cents. Offering him a tight-lipped smile, she tells him she's sorry.

"It ain't my fault young man. I just work here."

He apologizes, makes his purchase and seeing as no one is behind him, leans closer and drops his line. She moves a short step back from him, gasps and holds her hands over her heart.

"Oh, my goodness. No, no, no... I don't know of anyone missing. I hope it *is* only a rumour."

She has a sudden thought and turns her head and looks at the wall clock. 12:35. Reminds her Tim hasn't showed up for work. Odd. He's never late.

"Well, I can tell you he's probably not missing but he's working the afternoon shift and is usually here by now."

"Who are you talking about?"

"Tim Grant, one of our employees."

Carter backs off as someone is behind him waiting to get served. He takes his notebook from his shirt pocket and jots down the name. The cashier sees him and shakes her head, her ponytail swinging.

"Don't you worry about Tim. I'm sure he'll show up any minute. He's a good fella."

She busies herself with a woman at the cash and when he replies, she waves him off without looking at him.

"I'll drop by later to see if Tim made it in."

He leaves the store, unwraps his sandwich and stands beside his borrowed auto. He takes a bite and observes a Dodge taking off from the store parking lot. But it's blue so he ignores the smoky wisps of exhaust following it. Leaning up against his own car, he finishes his sandwich and tosses the empty soda bottle the back floor; he'll get a penny off his next bottle. He decides to go to Shediac and ask around there.

Four miles up the road, the car he saw earlier leaving the store is parked on the side of the road on a long stretch, wooded on both sides. An old logging road on the right is the only blemish on the long stretch. Unused now, it's overgrown with short shrubs and saplings. The hardwoods can't decide what to wear, their summer frocks of green or autumn reds and yellows. Carter has to wait until a dump truck goes by on the narrow road before he can pass the stopped car. Gazing out his side window, he can't help noticing the terrible paint job. It looks like it was painted by brush. He sees a man with his head looking down at something in the seat next to him. Carter assumes it's a map and thinks maybe he should see if the person is lost. He pulls over in front of the car.

Iron Spear looks up and couldn't be happier. Back at the store, he heard the young man asking about missing people. He had intended to follow him but this is perfect.

23

2:57 pm

Skip's boat is accelerating at its top speed of fifteen knots. The prow sluices through the water like a bully yelling get out of my way. Skip has a firm grip on the helm as he leans in closer to the window to study the shore. He stays well off the dunes that separate Bouctouche and the open strait and moves closer to shore when he goes past St. Edouard and slows the craft. His eyes dart back and forth along the section of wooded shore. His face is contorted in concentration. No matter how many times he's passed these shores, he's missed it before. Kravchenko is beside him, back in the seat, binoculars roaming to and fro.

"What should I be looking for?"

"You see the cliffs all along and dead trees as tall as a man's shoulders, the dirt all washed away from under them? There should be three, crisscrossed. Not far after that."

Kravchenko pays attention to the shore, to trees or logs sticking out from the soil, upturned roots, heads buried in the sand or bashed up on solid rock battered from wind and ice. A fair distance ahead he sees three long slender ones slumbering on the sand atop each other. Dropping the binoculars, he points to the spot.

"There, Skip. Maybe five hundred yards. Some trees look they're clinging to each other."

"Right you are. I see it now. Good eye."

Skip lowers the throttle to half speed and he soon slows before pointing the prow toward the shore. Kravchenko's chin drops and he grips the dash. He's about to question the Skip's judgement when he sees the illusion unfold. The shoreline to the right is identical to the shoreline to the left with the same cliff and flora. But it is set back thirty feet and opens inward to a shallow cove long enough and wide enough to hold fifty boats like Skip's. The perimeter consists of mostly cliffs and trees. No roads exist on the shoulders. The boat is now down to a putter barely above idle. Kravchenko's mouth is agape at how clever the hiding spot is. It's big enough to hide a warship.

"This is indeed a good hiding spot, Skip. Too bad there's nobody hiding. How deep is it here? You not worried about touching bottom?"

"Not sure exactly. But the government fellas tell us at low tide it's still almost a hundred feet and like a huge channel. A freak of nature they say, cut a million years ago. I'd say more likely the bottom was only muck and cruddy stone and that centuries of ice and waves and nasty storms took it all away. But they're supposed to know it all."

Skip shrugs and lets the boat idle, putting the transmission in neutral. It stops its forward motion and gently rocks with the pulse of the outgoing tide.

"Excuse me, Soldier, but seein' as we're all men here, hope you don't mind my indiscretion."

With that, Kravchenko watches him saunter to the stern where the backboard is lower and narrower. Skip props his knees against the wood and reaches for his zipper. Kravchenko frowns and turns to look at the shore. He hears the trickle of the man's relief and wishes the boat was in gear. He'd pay the man back by revving the boat and tossing him in. The image of Skip going headfirst in the drink with his dick in his hands makes him start laughing. Skip doesn't know why but starts chuckling too when they're both startled by a thump on the keel.

24

Same time

Unterseeboot 498 sits on the bottom of a deep-water canyon which runs into the shore to form a unique hiding spot. At night the U-boat can surface and recharge her batteries. It can't stay submerged for long durations. Its advance direction finding can detect surface ships and targets but is rarely used by *Oberleutnant Zur See* Werner Atzinger, the commander of the submarine, because it may alert enemy ships to its presence. He witnessed two ships at anchor. Freighters. What worries him is the armed trawler he saw yesterday. He identified it as a mine sweeper. And it's been hanging around.

After sending a radio message last night to his contact on land, the man he was sent to pick up, he retreated to this small cove to hide until the rendezvous at midnight on Saturday, two days away. He has men on shore hiding in the wooded area surrounding the inlet when sitting on the surface during the day like it was a short time ago. A warning had come in of a fishing boat plying the waters and sailing in his direction. A klaxon sounded inside the claustrophobic interior. Atzinger issued orders to his men.

"To battle stations. Submerge, submerge."

Inside the narrow control room, filled with gauges, dials, conduits, pipes and control valves, the men who drive the boat work in unison. Ballast tanks are filled and the submarine sinks to the bottom. She sits there for thirty minutes in total silence. There is no way of knowing if she was discovered. Atzinger is not a patient man. He commands his ship with the philosophy that the best defense is offense. He knows the bowl they are in is almost thirty meters deep.

"Let's take a look. Take us to seven meters. Up periscope."

There are two periscopes on the U-boat, one for observation and navigation, the second an attack periscope used for spotting and targeting enemy ships on the horizon. They work in tandem. Everyone goes still when they hear, or in this case feel, the periscope hit something. It keeps extending.

"Down periscope. Dive. Dive. Dive. Take us to thirty meters and full astern. Prepare torpedo one."

A voice over the intercom verifies torpedo one is ready to fire.

When the submarine moves off five hundred feet from shore, Atzinger calls an all-stop and orders them back to periscope depth. The commander sees the tail end of the fishing boat, adjusts its magnification, and reads, *Terese*, in red slanted script. Its bearing is due north, moving away from them. He's been holding his breath and relaxes as he scans the area for any other threats. Seeing none, he orders the boat back to its resting spot to wait.

25

Skip almost loses his balance when the boat rocks from whatever hit it and has to grab the side gunnel to stop from falling in. He dribbles on his dungarees and curses. Kravchenko catches himself by holding onto the cabin frame. The boat moves sideways for several feet and settles. Both men look over the side to see what is going on. Neither can see clearly as the waters are dark and share nothing. Skip moves back to the wheelhouse and puts the craft in reverse. Backing off, he notices something disappear into the froth but not before he can make it out.

"What do you see, Skip?"

"Looked like the tip of a fin from a large fish but I haven't a clue what would come this close to shore and be large enough to rock my boat."

"A whale maybe?"

"Maybe, but I doubt it. Let's motor out of here. Nothing else to see anyway."

"Yes, I need to get back to the base right away."

Skip pilots the boat north. Kravchenko is staring back at the cove. His mind goes on alert, thinking back to his earlier thought. Submarine! The hint of an enemy this close prickles his skin, pulls it tight across his brow. He mustn't say anything to Skip and contact the *Baffin* ASAP. Neither man have any idea how close they came to being blasted out of the water.

26

1:16 pm

Carter approaches the car with trepidation, watching the man closely, wary of strangers because of what has been happening. Yet he would never pass up a chance to help someone out. With a car approaching from Scoudouc, he drops his guard and taps on the window. The man looking back at him is older, eyes set far apart. He looks familiar. When he rolls down the window, Carter can see the unfolded map on the passenger's seat.

"Are you lost, Mister?"

"Well not really lost young man, only trying to decide the best route to Memramcook. Perhaps you can help me."

"I'm not too familiar with the area around Memramcook but I've been there before. If you show me your map, I can point out the quickest route."

He steps closer when a car speeds by with three young ladies inside. They toot the horn and wave at him. He hasn't a clue who it is but waves back out of politeness. He has a good look at the blonde on the passenger's side. What a cutie! The man inside the car is fumbling with the door handle.

"Wonderful. Let me get out and we can spread this map out on the hood."

Carter steps back from the vehicle and walks to the front. The man is close behind him and when Carter turns, he sees the map still lying in the front seat. He's about to point it out when he sees the scowl on the man's face and a gun pointing at his gut. Carter's eyes go wide and he stares at the man, open-mouthed. His heart starts racing and he gulps in fear when the man gives him a command.

"Move off to the opening in the woods."

"Listen, Mister... if...if you're planning on robbing me, I've got about fifteen dollars to my name and you can have it. No need for a gun."

The man slashes the barrel of the gun across Carter's cheek, making a gash along the jaw. Carter reacts with a yelp and his hands go to his face. He's too angry to be scared and remembers his hand-to-hand combat training. Before the man can recover from the swing, Carter lashes with his right and knocks the gun from the man's hand. Iron Spear didn't expect such a reaction from the scrawny kid. He steps forward and kicks Carter in the crotch. Carter goes to the ground, holding his testicles and cursing at the man. Recovering his gun, he kicks Carter in the side. He notices another car approaching from the Scoudouc direction and yells at Carter.

"Get up now! Move into the woods or I'll shoot you right here."

Carter moans as he tries to stand, the pain in his crotch starting to subside. He knows better than to resist with a gun pointing at him. He'll comply until he has a chance to overtake him. By the time another car goes by, they can't be seen when they are on the ditch side of the road. He wants to wave out for it to stop but instead he staggers along into the gap in the woods. After twenty feet in, the overgrown trail sweeps to the left. When they are out of sight, he tells Carter to stop.

"Turn around. Why are you asking about missing people back at the store?"

Now Carter remembers where he saw the man. He was buying cigarettes. He becomes emboldened by the man's request.

"What's it to you? Are you the one that left the bodies behind? You won't last long. You should give yourself up and the law might go easy on you."

"Answer me. Why are you looking for missing people?"

Carter has no doubt in his mind that this is the man who did the killing. He knows he's done for. He talks low, his head down, searching for a weapon of some sort. He sees a dead branch by his left foot. It's hidden from the man by tall grass.

"There was a body buried in the field by the Air Force base and I'm working with..."

He's been digging the toe of his boot under the branch and when he feels it move, he kicks out and the branch catches his assailant in the chest. Dirt and dried bark hit him in the face. He sees Carter make a move toward him and shoots wildly. Two shots. One goes over Carter's left shoulder and the other hits him in the chest. The impact knocks Carter to the ground, his head bouncing off a stump. Iron Spear stares at the inert body, watching blood from the chest wound colour the shirt red. He pockets the gun and drags the body into a cluster of small brush.

Returning to the highway and the other car, he finds the keys in the ignition. He reverses it and drives it into the rutted road, the bottom making scraping sounds as he maneuvers it around the bend and stops. Checking that it can't be seen from the road, he chucks the keys in the woods and leaves. He has no remorse, only a feeling of security that one more obstacle is out of the way. He carries on to the hardware store in Moncton where he needs some things for his planned caper Saturday night. More importantly, he has to case out Albright's Quarry and Construction. He needs dynamite.

27

Entry to the main office building on the base is through two wide glass doors which are locked after 6:30 and manned on the inside by private security personnel, In this case, an older gentleman from Diamond Security Services, distinguished by a bushy moustache and thick grey hair swept back from an elongated forehead. When Kravchenko knocks on the glass to catch the man's attention, he's informed he missed Group Captain Clark by fifteen minutes. Not sure what to do, he hastens to the building where the magnetron is stored. When he arrives, he's greeted by an armed Corporal of the Service Police who is stationed at the guard house.

"Good evening, Corporal. Is all good here?"

The man snaps a smart salute for the warrant officer.

"Yes, Sir. There's been lots of activity today but only with approved personnel going in and out. Nothing amiss. My partner is doing a perimeter check as we speak. I'm in direct communication with the guards inside and we cross check each other on the half hour. AC1 Cronin confirms all is quiet."

"Has Sergeant Booth or Carter been around lately?"

"Sergeant Booth is inside now, sir. No sign of Carter."

"Thank you, Corporal. As you were."

Kravchenko shows his ID to the Corporal, who checks his list and nods a go ahead. Inside the door, his ID is double checked by AC1

Cronin who informs him Sergeant Booth is in the conference room. When Kravchenko enters the room, Sgt. Booth stands at attention and salutes.

Booth can see something is troubling the warrant officer by the look on his face.

"Good afternoon, Sir. Or should I say good evening? How did it go on the boat?"

"I appreciate you staying later, Sergeant. Before I answer your question, have you spoken to GC Clark before he left? I tried his home phone but there is no answer and the main office is closed up.,"

"No Sir, I haven't. May I ask what's going on?"

"I can't confirm it, Booth, but out on the water I think we may have come in contact with something we shouldn't have, and I get an eerie feeling it might be a submarine."

Booth scowls with angry eyes. The enemy so close!

"A submarine? How can that be? If I remember correctly, a sub hunter is trolling the waters around the coast. Wouldn't they have detected it?"

"Depends on how experienced and level-headed the sub commander is as well as the captain of the sub hunter ship. I was hoping to contact the ship which I remember as being the *Baffin* but I'm not sure if I have the authority. It should be the GC."

"But if you suspect one, shouldn't we be informing them?"

"Well, this is it, Booth. I don't have proof. But something connected with the boat when we were floating in a small cove, a very deep cove the owner of the boat informed me. It could've been a large fish or a seal or a dolphin but it's a gut feeling I have, knowing the magnetron is here. The fact that it's top secret, and with the dead bodies... I'm not sure. I think it best for the GC to make the call."

Booth nods in agreement, knowing of the GC's insistence on keeping this quiet.

"Pardon me for saying, Sir, but he's only been posted here for a short time. If we solve this, he'll look good. I can understand with what we're hiding here, we should keep everything on base. He has faith in you, sir."

"Thanks, Sergeant. What you say has merit. By the way, where's Carter?"

"Not sure, Sir. I last spoke to him this morning after he changed out of his uniform and asked me for a lift to his buddy's place down the road. I dropped him off there and have been busy with my searches."

Kravchenko gets an uncomfortable feeling. Maybe it's nothing but Carter comes across as the kind of person to follow orders. A glance at the wall clock tells him it's almost seven.

"Sergeant Booth, if Carter is not back when we're finished, have two men search the base, check his friend's place, check the community. Did you see the vehicle he was using?"

"There was only one car. A '37 Ford, five-window coupe. Dark green. Smart looking car but it needed a wash and the back bumper is missing. Couldn't see the front or the other side. I assume it would be that one."

"Look after that, Sergeant."

"I'll look after it personally, Sir, unless you have other orders."

Kravchenko likes this man. The grit in Booth's eyes and the determination in his stance is a convincing sight. He looks after his people.

"Good idea, Booth. Thank you. Ok, let's sit down and you can tell me what you have."

The conference room is centered with a circular table surrounded by ten chairs all tucked in at attention. They each pull out one directly across from each other. Writing tablets are piled in the center of the table along with a metal cup containing pencils and a screwdriver. Booth takes out the notepad from his jacket pocket. He flips through and studies a page midway before relating his findings.

"I contacted every police station in a wide radius as you ordered and this is what I found."

Booth ticks off the twenty-three stations and what districts they covered. He was met with caution and before they would commit to anything he always had to explain the reason for his inquiry. He told them he was with the Public Relations. The Air Force was committed to serving the local constabulary with any manpower they may need in searches. Most of them had no such cases. But three of them do. One of them is a female. One of the two males is only twelve but the other one is interesting.

"... Amherst, the first town in Nova Scotia across our border from Aulac had a request three days ago. Male, twenty-seven years old. Name's Bert Downes. Last seen leaving work Saturday night at 5:30. Works at an Irving service station. Still missing."

He looks at Kravchenko to see what he's thinking, watching him doodle on one of the tablets as he listens.

"It's a possibility, Sir."

"Yes, it could be. Is that all they gave you? No physical measurements or distinguishing features?"

"It was the only information the man was authorized to give me, and this was the Deputy Chief. I tried to use the GC's muscle but I was told to have the GC contact them."

"Tomorrow, I want you down there, as early as your duties will allow you. Let them have their coffee first. Go over his head and talk to the chief. I'll get the GC to give him a call while you're on your way. Try and get a picture."

"Yes, Sir. That's about it. It's not much I'm afraid."

"It is something and had to be done, Sergeant. Good work. We could be on to an identity. We don't have many leads forward. The car he could be using. Boot prints. Which reminds me that's Carter not here. He was supposed to compare them to the boots in Hangar Five..."

Kravchenko pauses, something in his gut tells him Carter could be in trouble from nosing around today.

"This is starting to worry me, Booth. It might be best if you get on with your search for Carter. I'm going to contact Collins in Winnipeg. He should still be around given the time difference. Keep me posted."

"Yes, Sir."

Booth replaces his jacket from the back of the chair and dons his hat. Kravchenko watches him leave, deep into his own thoughts. If his gut feeling is correct and there is a submarine offshore lurking in the deeps undetected. It is there for a reason and the only one which makes sense is the magnetron, either to steal it away or for someone to escape by. On his way out he'll tell the guards to remain totally alert. He has only until tomorrow morning until the GC decides to get the police involved. Given the man's obsession for secrecy, Kravchenko resolves to insist on taking that move if the GC wants to continue putting them off.

It's a decision neither Kravchenko nor Group Captain Clark will have to make.

28

2:30 pm Four hours earlier.

Jeb Stuart turned sixteen today. He had to wait until after lunch for his father to drive him into Moncton where he bought his first hunting license for small game like rabbit, partridge, and pheasant. Holding it in his hands, his skinny face was split with a toothful smile. He's never felt so grown up. On top of that his parents let him take the day off from school and gave him a new red and black checked hunting jacket. His sister gave him a hunting knife, a shiny six-inch blade holstered in a stiff leather sheath. After a pat on the back from his father, they drove to Scoudouc where Jeb's best friend, Bobby Hudson lives. They're going hunting partridge this afternoon.

Jeb jumps out of the car and grabs the shotgun and shells from the back seat.

"Thanks, Dad."

"Be careful, Son. You have been given a privilege and I expect you to be wise with it. You do what Bobby tells you. He's smart with a gun. Good luck and I'll pick you up around six.

"Yep, see you then."

Jeb is greeted in the front yard by Bobby who is a good six inches taller and stockier with straight dark, slicked back hair full of Brylcreem. He's trying to grow a moustache but the only evidence of one is a dark fuzz on his upper lip. Jeb tells him it looks silly but Bobby thinks it makes him look older and the girls like older guys, so... He turned sixteen in the spring and already has his driver's license. He quit school last year, works at the White Rose service station in Scoudouc and he gets Sunday and Monday off. He recently bought a '31 Chevrolet, which keeps making unusual sounds and conking out, but he loves it and keeps it shiny around the rust spots.

"Hey Jeb. That's your old man's shotgun. It's new, ain't it?"

"Yeah, it is. Winchester semi-automatic, 12 gauge. He bought it last year when they first came out. You ready to go?"

"Sure am. Let's get a move on."

The boys jump in the black and rust Chevrolet. The guns sit in the back seat. Bobby is using his father's Savage Fox, a 16-gauge shotgun. He lives on the northern portion of the village beyond the Air Force base. They are heading toward Moncton. Jeb is itching to get into the woods and has a prickly feeling on his neck when he thinks of bagging his first bird. He's shot the gun before. He remembers his father teaching him to aim for the head, not the body or it will be too full of lead to eat.

"Where are we going?"

"My uncle owns a stretch of woods along the road here, about four or five miles from Leblanc's store. There's an old logging road. It don't get used very much now. My grandfather was a logger. Made his living cutting wood. But he's been dead over fifteen years ago and stopped using it even before then. Should be clear enough."

"Oh boy, I can hardly wait."

The two hunters reach the wooded area ten minutes later. Bobby parks his car near a narrow gap in the forest off the main road. They get their guns out and stand at the front of the car, looking into the overgrown trail. Bobby points at the tire tracks in front.

"Looks like somebody drove their car in here. The marks don't look old, maybe today. Hope nobody is in there now."

"Yeah, we might have to shoot them."

Bobby looks at his friend with a questioning brow until he sees the grin and they both start laughing.

"Right. We'll have to shoot them. Damn trespassers. C'mon, let's go and remember to be quiet."

They walk abreast, one in each wheel rut. Jeb is pointing to the big maple tree at the turn of the bend with a rust and red umbrella.

"All right. Wow, the trees sure are pretty, turning all kinds of nice colors."

"Pretty? Trees don't get pretty, they get beautiful. It's my favorite time of the ..."

Jeb is on the left side and they stop dead when they round the crook in the road. A car is parked in their way. They approach it in silence, looking around for people. Jeb sees something odd.

"Oh, shit Bobby, a pair of boots are sticking out of those shrubs and there's somebody in them."

The boys hold up their guns and tread easy toward the boots. Seeing Carter lying there with a bloody shirt, they both go white in the face and gawk at each other. Bobby sets down his gun and kneels by the body. He reaches for the neck to search for a pulse.

"Is he dead, Bobby?"

"No, no he's not but his heartbeat is really weak."

"What are we gonna do?"

"There's a lot of blood on his shirt. We better get him to a hospital right away and we'd better call the police."

"Shouldn't we call the police first?"

Bobby is thinking hard, staring at the man's face.

"It looks like he bled a lot. There's an infirmary at the Air Force base. My aunt is a nurse there, she might be there today. It's closer than the city hospital in Moncton. Set your gun down and grab his feet."

Bobby pushes some brush aside and stands at Carter's head, grabbing him under the arms. Jeb takes him by the knees and the boys carry him to the Chevrolet and maneuver him into the back seat. Carter lost consciousness when his head hit a stump and is awakening. He moans and grabs the side of his chest where the bullet went through.

"Hang in there, Mister. We'll get you to a hospital."

Carter, delirious and weak with so much blood lost, passes out again.

"Go get our guns, Jeb and I'll turn the car around."

"Shouldn't we call the police?"

"We don't have time right now but we will. Hurry."

Jeb is back in two minutes and gets into the already moving car. Bobby has the gas pedal to the mat and the car is coughing and jerking as if getting too much fuel.

"C'mon, you stupid car, act right."

He slaps the steering wheel and the car, reacting like it's been chastised, comes to life and speeds along the road. At sixty miles an hour, it only takes them five minutes to get to the White Rose where Bobby spies a co-worker pumping gas. He brings the car to a skidding stop, raising dust in the yard. Danny, the guy pumping gas, jolts back and stares googly-eyed at the car which stops three feet in front of him. Through the open car window Bobby yells.

"Danny. Call the police. Somebody got shot. Going to the infirmary on the base. Hurry up."

Bobby doesn't wait for an acknowledgement but carries on to the roadway, wheels spinning and ass swinging. It takes less than a minute to reach the entrance into the base. The car screeches to a halt at the guard house. Bobby calls out to the man standing outside, gesturing with a pointed thumb to the wounded man in the back seat. The sentry is AFC 2 Dominic Belliveau and he recognizes Carter. He waves to the other airman in the shack.

"Open up the gate and be quick, Daryll. It's Carter and he's injured. Call the infirmary and let them know he's coming."

He collects the shotguns from the floor of the back seat.

"We'll hang on to these until you return."

Pointing down the main road, he directs Bobby where to go.

"Pull up front and honk your horn."

Bobby bypasses the first two hangars and turns left. The infirmary is the second building on the right. He comes to a halt and lays on the horn. People are already staring at the car that came speeding onto the base and watch with astonished looks at the commotion. A man in an orderly's uniform comes running out.

"What's going on, boys?"

"We found this guy in the woods, Mister. He's in bad shape."

Sergeant Ernest Chiasson checks the pulse and shakes his head at the man's pallor. He shouts out to a woman standing at the open door.

"Get a stretcher, Miss Weatherby, quickly!"

He opens the victim's shirt to examine the wound and is pleased to see it's not in the center of the chest but off to the side. The entry wound is shrunken to a pucker in the skin, three inches down from the clavicle. He's seen enough bullet wounds to know it won't be the same with the exit wound. He's hoping it was small caliber.

Another orderly rushes out with a stretcher along an inclined ramp on the left of the building. The nurse is Bobby's aunt and waves to him with a surprised look on her face. Sergeant Chiasson helps the other medic. During the movement, Carter regains consciousness. His eyes are glazed and he stares unfocused into the sergeant's face. He strains to talk and can only muster a voice shy of a whisper.

"K... Kravchenk, warring oshifer..."

Chiasson registers it in his mind, he understands. Warrant Officer. Not sure what Kravchenk means. Keeping this man alive is his first responsibility.

"Stand aside boys. Follow the lady back in and tell her where you found him."

Chiasson takes the stretcher by the head and together he and the other orderly go in the side door. It's being held by another man. Chiasson is already barking out orders to call Dr. Delaney and prepare surgery.

Jeb and Bobby have been standing at the front of Bobby's car watching the action in a state of fascination, their eyes big and full of relief. The nurse calls to them.

"Bobby, bring your chum and come inside."

Jeb elbows his buddy.

"No hunting today, I guess. Oh well, it feels good to be rescuing somebody, don't it?"

"Yeah, yeah it does. Who do you think shot him, Bobby?"

"I don't know, Jeb, but they ain't friendly whoever they are. I sure hope they can fix him up. C'mon, this is Aunt Maggie."

The boys tell what happened. Carter gets blood transfusions and is patched up. Chiasson only gets a chance to find out who Kravchenko is after the operation where he was assisting the doctor. At seven thirty he contacts the officer on duty, who informs him from the list of personnel, a Warrant Officer Stefan Kravchenko is with the Service Police and is on base at present. He assured Sergeant Chiasson he would have him located and informed.

By the time Kravchenko arrives at the infirmary, he'll be greeted by a detective who is not happy.

29

Warrant Officer Blaine Collins of the Winnipeg Service Police is being most cooperative. He states that they are no closer to an answer today of who murdered Coleman than they were when they found the body. But there are interesting notes which catch Kravchenko's attention. Coleman was found murdered from a knife to the chest. Kravchenko poked him for more details and discovered the same type of stroke was used there as in these New Brunswick murders. Perhaps it was a technique learned at the same training program, something both warrant officers feel is most likely given the distance apart. But nothing can be eliminated.

An additional fact is Coleman worked in Supply and had access to uniforms. Collins mentions Coleman was under observation almost a year ago for missing supplies. Rumour had it that he was stealing and selling goods on the black market but it could not be proved. He was never caught. Another serviceman was apprehended and the matter dropped.

Something else Collins mentions, and he is specific in keeping it quiet, is that when the Service Police gained entry to Coleman's off-base apartment, a balled-up piece of paper found under the chesterfield had a name and long-distance phone number for the Toronto area. The name is Smythe and the phone number is disconnected. Using his contacts, he discovered the number was originally issued to a company called Global

Freight which does not exist anywhere he looked. Another dead end.

Before they end the call, Collins informs Kravchenko of his intentions.

"We found fingerprints other than Coleman's at the apartment. Not sure where it will take us but they could be from the killer. If I get anything else, I'll let you know."

"Same here and thank you, Blaine."

Kravchenko disconnects and is studying his notes when the phone rings. Glancing up at the wall clock he sees it's a little after eight o'clock. He picks up the receiver.

"Kravchenko here."

"Good evening, Warrant Officer Kravchenko. This is Lieutenant Conrad Forden, OOW, speaking. I received a call from Segreant Chiasson who wanted me to convey you the following message. *It is urgent you proceed to the infirmary as soon as possible. A recovering serviceman is asking for you.*"

Kravchenko thinks of Carter right away.

"Is it AC2 Jeremy Carter, Sir? And recovering from what?"

"Yes, it is. I haven't been informed of the extent of his wounds other than it is not life threatening."

Kravchenko sighs with relief but hangs his head, lips pressed in regret. He shouldn't have sent the boy out alone and unarmed to ask questions. Thankful he's still alive. The damn war is closer than people think!

"Are you still there?"

Kravchenko snaps out of his guilt.

"Has Sergeant Booth been informed?"

"I can't verify that, but I'll find him and tell him right away."

"Thank you, Lieutenant. I'll be right over."

"One other thing, Kravchenko. There is a member of the Mounted Police Force here as well. Be warned, she's in a foul mood."

"She?"

"Yes, not common, I know, but with so many men at war, there are

103

more female police officers these days and this one seems capable. Might be wise to get here as soon as you can."

"Thank you again, Lieutenant."

Kravchenko hangs up and curses and talks to the empty room.

"Damn, I was hoping to be better prepared when the GC informed the police. I wish I could speak to him first but still no answer on his phone. Where is he?"

30

8:32 pm

Kravchenko speaks to the two guards on the way out to be extra alert, keep eyes everywhere. He told them to report anything, with emphasis on *anything*, unusual to him ASAP. After informing them of his destination, he sets off at a brisk pace breathing in the cooler air. He's tired. It's been a long day. He needs a shower, a shave and to change his uniform. Thinking of what he's uncovered so far, he feels like a guy stuck in the mud, wheels spinning. Carter's in hospital. He's getting nowhere and now the police. A foul mood, indeed! Well, *he's* in a foul mood too. It takes Kravchenko less than ten minutes to reach the infirmary.

Getting directions from a reception desk, Kravchenko removes his hat and searches out the recovery area. A long hallway separates a variety of rooms: administration and staff room on one side and registration, triage, examination rooms and utilities opposite. Patient rooms and surgery take up the back. Nurses rush about with charts or trays. Their long white dresses and dainty caps identify their responsibilities. Doctors in white lab coats, stethoscopes entwined about their shirt collar, go from room to room. Custodians clean everything twenty-four hours a day. At another counter, he finds it staffed by a nurse of ample girth. The buttoned-up blouse over her robust breasts makes her appearance seem matronly helped also by the oval framed glasses on the tip of her nose. She looks at him with her *what-now* face.

"Yes?"

"Aircraftsman 2 Jeremy Carter, please. Recovering from an operation."

She frowns at him and picking up a chart, flips down three pages. She checks it with darting eyes and looks up at him.

"What's your name?"

"Warrant Officer Stefan Kravchenko."

Another glance at the page.

"Right, then. I still need to see some ID?"

Kravchenko removes his Air Force identification from his wallet and passes it to her.

She checks the photo and looks back at him.

"I like you better without the moustache. Off you go then. Room 104. Ten minutes is all you have. He might even be sleeping and if so, leave him be. He only got out of the operation less than three hours ago."

She ignores him and returns to her desk. He walks through a wide door and into the back section. Not as busy here. 104 is the fourth and last room on the right. The door is closed. In front of it a woman is sitting forward on a hard backed wooden chair more suited to a desk, a note pad in her hands. She remains oblivious to the few staff milling about. He watches her for a few moments. Her hair is tucked under her service cap, a few strands trying to escape in the back. She has a clear profile which reminds him of Ingrid Bergman. Her tunic fits her lithe frame in a flattering manner. The yellow stripe along the thigh and glossy boots seem at odds with the drab brown of her uniform. She doesn't look intimidating. She only looks up when Kravchenko is standing beside her.

"Hello. I'm Warrant Officer Stefan Kravchenko."

The RCMP officer stands and takes Kravchenko's outstretched hand. The first thing Kravchenko notices is the appealing blue of her eyes, which makes him think of a clear sky. A pert nose, clear tawny skin and heart shaped face make her attractive without any hint of naivete. He guesses her to be close to his age. The look on her face tells him she's upset.

"Good evening, Officer. I'm Inspector Dia Francis and I think you had better fill me in on what's going on here."

"Please call me Stefan. May I call you Dia?"

"No, you may not. It's Inspector Francis."

"Fair enough then, Inspector. Is AC Carter awake? Have you spoken to him?"

"No, and yes. He's not awake and I spoke to him briefly before he nodded off. He was a tad delirious but awake enough to mention a body with no head he discovered three days ago. Why weren't the police informed before today?"

"A good question Inspector. I am ready to explain everything but can we go somewhere else more conducive to your inquiry? The cafeteria runs twenty-four hours and we can grab a coffee or tea if you prefer and I'll fill you in."

Francis relaxes slightly, she was expecting the same kind of resistance she received from the hospital staff who informed her they were not authorized to share any information without the approval of their commanding officer, who at present is unavailable.

"Yes, I could use a coffee. It's been a long day."

"Me too."

He turns to lead her out of the infirmary and two buildings away to the kitchen and mess. They walk in silence with the inspector taking in the man beside her. When she looked into his dark eyes, her initial bad mood softened. She could see kindness and no resistance. It's tough enough being a female officer in a man's world and being soft never got her anywhere. Her first reaction is always to be tough. She is slightly off guard at his good looks. She shrugs off her feelings and is about to follow him in, when he stops to hold the door open for her and tips his head for her to go first. At least he has manners she thinks. When they enter, he points to an empty table along the right wall of the mess.

"What would you like in your coffee, and would you like one of the cinnamon rolls if there are any left? They're quite delicious, made this morning."

She feels a pang in her stomach at the mention of food. She's not had anything to eat since she had a banana in the afternoon.

"Black, please, and yes to the cinnamon roll."

"I'll be right back."

He returns in a few moments holding a tray with two steaming mugs, two forks and two dessert plates holding cinnamon rolls oozing with dark creamy filing. Setting it in the middle of the table, he takes his own mug and plate and sits opposite her. He notices she has a notepad the same as his, open to a blank page with a mechanical pencil sitting beside it. She doesn't say anything until she has a sip of the hot coffee and a bite of the dessert.

"OK, Kravchenko, fill me in but first I'd like an explanation for the delay in notifying us. Were you going to?"

"Yes, of course. When the first body was discovered..."

"First body? You mean there is more than one?"

He nods while taking another bite.

"Two. Upon discovery, our commanding officer, Group Captain Clark, pointed out that they were found on Air Force property and there are things going on here, Inspector, which are not meant to be disclosed. With the war raging, Air Force Base Scoudouc is participating in a highly sensitive activity which cannot go beyond our doors. Very few people are involved. At the time I was brought in, he felt it best if we could solve the murders and present it to the authorities as a *fait accompli*. Keep it contained as much as possible. I was given until tomorrow morning before we would call you folks."

She's halfway through her cinnamon roll, and a pastry flake sits on her chin. Kravchenko finds it endearing. He mimics wiping his chin with his napkin and a nod to her.

"Can I inquire what the sensitive activity is?" she asks.

"You can certainly inquire but you would have to ask the GC."

"Is he available?"

"Oddly enough he has been incommunicado all evening. I myself have been trying to reach him unsuccessfully. The night officer on call is Squadron Leader Aldous Hinchey but he is not in the loop. GC Clark must be detained by another important matter but I have let the duty officer know I am looking for him and to keep trying to reach him."

She finishes her roll and wipes her fingers with her napkin and Kravchenko can't help but admire the sensuous lips, how full and pink they are. He admonishes himself for being so easily distracted and tells himself to pay attention.

"What are your credentials, Kravchenko? Why are you leading this... internal investigation, and have you solved it yet?"

"Before signing up, I was a police officer in Manitoba and..."

He goes on to relay what has happened since he's been called in. Spending the next fifteen minutes, he relates what he's discovered and the fact that he has got nowhere. When he tells her of the unidentified radio signal and his foray along the coast this afternoon, he doesn't mention his suspicions of a submarine, wanting to discuss it with the GC first.

".. and I am no further ahead on identifying the bodies and now I have a wounded comrade and a killer on the loose."

"Do you suspect the killings related to this sensitive activity going on here?"

"At this point, yes, I do."

"What's your next step?"

He shakes his head, pushes his empty cup and plate away from him and sits back.

"I need to identify the bodies and am at a roadblock. I'm hoping the identity will lead me further. I have a lead on a car and a false identity."

"Where are the bodies now?"

"On ice in one of our hangers."

Inspector Francis sits back as well and with her head down, Kravchenko realizes she too is pondering her next move.

"Ok, here's what we're going to do."

"We?"

"Yes, we. I'm taking charge of the investigation. I will do you the honour of letting you stick by my side and to be honest, I can use your expertise. I respect the fact you are, or were, a fellow police officer. I am going to have the bodies sent to the morgue and have the coroner and pathologist arrange for a viewing and to do their tricks. Maybe find some more clues."

"I'm not sure that's a good idea, Inspector."

"I believe that's my call, Kravchenko, not yours or the Air Force."

As much as he likes the woman, he's not going to be overridden without the GC knowing and authorizing any action.

"I'm afraid it isn't your call, Inspector. Do I need to remind you there is a war raging in Europe and we are the good guys? This needs to be discussed and okayed by my commanding officer. Right now, that looks like it might only be possible tomorrow morning at O-seven hundred hours. That's seven in the morning to you civilians, when the GC reports for work."

He can tell she's miffed but he doesn't care. He has his orders and she will have to abide by them for the time being. She sighs and stares at him with frost in her eyes but realizes she won't get any further without his cooperation. She responds gruffly.

"Okay, there's nothing we can do tonight. I'll be here at the front gate at six-forty-five tomorrow morning and I expect whoever is manning the gate will know I'm coming."

She stands and slides her chair back. Kravchenko gathers the cups and plates back on the tray and nods to her.

"Fair enough, Inspector."

Dia realizes she doesn't need to be so sharp with the man. As one police officer to another, she knows he's as concerned as she is.

"I apologize for being so curt but I get pushed around so much for being a woman and a First Nations. I don't like it. I'm tired and to be honest when I get this way, I tend to be a bit cranky."

"I don't prejudge people. Neither of the things you mentioned ever crossed my mind. Everyone has to prove their worth to me, male or female. And honestly, I'm done in too. I'll feel a lot better in the morning. We can meet at the gate and then we'll go to see Group Commander Clark."

She sees he's serious and not patronizing her. She offers her first smile, even though its tight-lipped and weak.

"Yeah, that uniform is kind of wrinkled, by the way. Looks like you've been sleeping in it."

Looking himself over, he sees what she sees and starts laughing.

"It does, doesn't it? In the morning then, Inspector. We'll get things in order and solve this. Can you find your way back to your vehicle?"

"Yes, I can, thank you and good night."

He moves to return the tray to the drop off area when she stops and calls out to him.

"Oh wait, I meant to give you this."

She holds out another note pad.

"The orderly gave me this. It was found in Carter's jacket and I commandeered it. It's your comrade's notebook."

He acknowledges her offer with a curious look in his eyes and takes it. Before she turns to leave, she ups the ante from the last attempt and smiles wider.

"And please, call me Dia."

31

Iron Spear parks his car in a cut-off a quarter mile from the quarry. With the lights out, he drives the vehicle down a rutted road until he is certain it cannot be seen from the road. It's pitch dark and he's not too worried. The quarry is five miles away from the nearest house in a valley cut by the Rousseau River, a feeder to the much larger Petitcodiac River. Closing the car door, he makes sure he has his flashlight in his pocket and a crowbar. Looking up at the sky all he sees is a sliver of moon and a dark plateau full of pinpoints of light. A bluish-grey pall makes easy going.

He was here earlier when the quarry was full of activity and cruised right up to the scales where he told the man he was a sales agent for Dominion Explosives and wondered if he could speak to the foreman. Wearing a suit and tie, a fake moustache, glasses, and a wig of longer hair, he looked nothing like the man who left work at the Scoudouc Air Force base at midnight. He's a carpenter, one of the many civilians working on base. He changed his shifts with Marc-Denis. Everything's going according to plan. He only had to find out where the dynamite is stored. The older man who he approached was happy to show him around, telling him his timing is good as the company is putting out tenders for a new shipment of dynamite and he even gave him the purchasing agent's names and office address in Moncton. Iron Spear discarded the information as soon as he left. He knows exactly where he needs to go.

Making his way down the dirt road, he comes to the entrance of the quarry. A tall wide gauge gate is across the road and the triangular shape of the *No Trespassing* sign is visible in the dim night light. He can't read it but knows what it says. The two gates are held together in the center by a chain held tight by a padlock. It only bars entrance for vehicles so he can squeeze past the edge on the right by stepping into a ditch which follows the road into the compound. The scale house is five hundred feet in. There is a ramp of packed gravel at both end of the scales, but another narrow road goes in beside it for vehicles not needing to be weighed.

He moves past the weighing station and carries on for another one-minute walk until he is in front of a group of low buildings on the left. They include a two-bay garage with doors big enough to admit the heavy equipment and trucks used in the crushing process, an administration office, a storeroom and at the very end, a nightwatchman's shanty. The roofline is silhouetted in the starry sky with right angles and slopes. There is a light on in the small window to the right of the door. To the far right, a dozen paces from the watchman's shack, is a solid building of concrete walls, maybe twenty feet by twenty feet, with a flat roof. A metal door bars entrance from the front and a heavy padlock holds it closed.

Movement in the guard's building causes him to duck down beside a Cleartrac crawler with one track missing. The mechanics were working on it when he visited. The watchman is donning a hat and buttoning up his coat as he leaves the shack. A flashlight with a powerful beam sweeps around the yard. Iron Spear watches him make his rounds, flashing the ray of light between the buildings, going inside each one and returning, crossing the road where several trucks are parked to inspect them. His last stop is the location Iron Spear is most interested in. The guard walks around the concrete structure, double checks the locked door and returns to his shanty. The German guesses he does his rounds every hour but as he is not sure, he hastens to the back of the buildings following the same path the watchman did until he is on the opposite side of the concrete structure where the foreman showed him his stock of dynamite.

Treading carefully, watching his step in the darkness, he arrives at the locked door. Remembering what he deemed the weakest spot where the hasp was attached to the jamb, he places the crowbar under the lip and pries. It is bolted stronger than he anticipated. He spends five minutes worrying the metal hasp until he has secure leverage, and using all his strength, he heaves his body upward and comes down on the prybar with all his force. The screws are embedded deep in the wood and scream as they are forced from their nest. In the eerie silence of the night, the noise seems as loud as a gunshot. The watchman heard it too.

Hustling from his shanty, the man bursts from the doorway with a baton in his hand and looks to his left by the dynamite storage room where the noise came from. His heavy flashlight scans the area around the structure and when he walks over to the door, he gasps at the hanging lock. A chill of dread passes through him and he flashes the light around. When he swings the beam toward the trucks, Iron Spear assails him from behind.

The ten-inch blade, sharper than a barber's razor, slices through the fabric of his jacket, shirt and undershirt and enters the left kidney, cutting muscle and sinew on the way in. The baton and light go to the ground and the watchman grunts and screeches into the night. Before he can react, Iron Spear delivers the deadly stroke. Blood spurts from the cut, covering the man's front and the dirt at their feet. The body goes flaccid and falls face first on the ground. He bends to pick up the flashlight. Pointing the beam at his knife, he grimaces at the blood and wipes his hands and knife on the jacket of the fallen man. He replaces the blade in the sheath strapped to his belt, sets the flashlight down and points the beam toward the concrete building. Grabbing the man under the arms, he tugs the body into the building, using his butt to push the door inward. The broken hasp and lock bang against the metal door but he pays no attention to the noise. He places the body against the wall to the left of the door where it rests lopsided. Using his own flashlight, he scans the boxes of dynamite and removes one stick. Although he knows dynamite needs a blasting cap, he handles it with great caution. Turning to a wall lined with a rough cabinet of drawers, he removes one detonator and a length of fuse. He knows from his own research, the fuse the quarry uses burns at thirty seconds per foot. He only needs twelve feet but takes fifteen to be sure.

Closing the door tightly behind him, he does his best to pound the hasp screws into the holes. Upon close inspection anyone will see it has been tampered with but otherwise, it looks intact. The only thing they will find missing is the night watchman.

32

Kravchenko is wakened by a gentle shake of his shoulder. He's in the Number 2 men's barracks, at the front by the main entrance. The room is in darkness with only the glimmer of a permanent light in the washroom at the opposite end of the building, shaded by the end wall.

"Warrant Officer, GC Clark requests your presence at oh six hundred at his office."

Kravchenko was in a deep sleep, a kaleidoscope of dreams alternating between headless bodies to Dia Francis and is relieved to be woken up. He blinks from the low light and recognizes LAC Lutes, Clark's assistant.

"Thank you. What time is it now?"

"Just a bit after five-thirty, Sir."

Kravchenko sits up on the edge of his cot, rubbing the sleep from his eyes, hair all mussed up, lines on his face from the scrunched-up pillow he was sleeping on.

"I'll be there, Lutes."

"Yes, Sir."

Kravchenko sits for a moment, head cradled in his hands with his elbows resting on his knees, letting his mind settle. His thoughts return to the inspector. Her image is as clear as it was when they parted at the cafeteria. The high cheekbones and the smile she left him with seem to be embedded in his brain. His heart beats faster and he shakes his head.

He whispers to himself.

"Better get those thoughts out of your head, Stefan."

Out of the blue, he feels melancholy. He's been dedicated to his work, so much that he never felt he had time for a relationship, and his longtime sweetheart of the past has found someone else while stationed in England. In her last letter in April, she told him she'd waited long enough for him to return her feelings and is moving on. She met another Canadian soldier while serving at the Birmingham #1 Canadian Hospital where she is a nurse in the Royal Canadian Medical Corps with the Surgical Field Unit. It hurt at first but has now settled into a sad memory. There has been no one else since, and he's never experienced an attraction as profound as he has to the inspector.

"Enough," he tells himself. He stands and takes his shaving kit, clean boxers, and T-shirt from the locker beside his bed, trying to tread quietly so as not to waken the ten others bunked with him. He heads for the shower, does a quick shampoo, soap down and rinse. He combs his hair, shaves, bundles up his used underclothing and puts his clean ones on. Returning to the locker, he puts on a clean work uniform with the short jacket, reminding himself to have the other dry cleaned as soon as possible. He straps on his sidearm. At 5:55 AM he enters the foyer to the main offices. Running up the stairs, he meets LAC Lutes at the man's desk which sits outside the closed door of Group Captain Clark's office.

"Warrant Officer Kravchenko reporting to Group Captain Clark."

"Please hold tight, Sir, and I'll let him know you're here."

"Thank you."

Kravchenko does not wait long. Lutes leaves the door open and waves him in.

"Can I get you a coffee, Sir?"

"Yes, please. Black and two sugars if you don't mind."

Kravchenko makes his way into the office to find Clark sitting in one of the two seats in front of his desk rather than behind it. He's wearing a lopsided smile and it takes Kravchenko by surprise. He's not sure why anyone would be in a good mood this early in the morning amid the confusion going on. Between the two seats there is a small table with an ashtray on it, an unlit pipe resting inside. A blue haze hovers near the ceiling and Kravchenko can still smell the sweet aroma of pipe tobacco. He wasn't aware that Clark smoked. Clark motions him to the other seat.

"Good morning, Warrant Officer Kravchenko. I understand you were trying to reach me last evening but I was detained..."

He pauses for a moment obviously to reflect on what he was doing and it makes his smile broader.

"... and I was informed we have an injured serviceman and that the police are now involved. I need you to fill me in on the police officer. Have you met the man, and what have you discussed?"

"It's actually a woman, Sir. Inspector Dia Francis. I explained what steps I've taken and I have not mentioned anything about the magnetron, only that the base was involved in sensitive issues. She wants to take over the investigation but I commented there were more serious matters at hand before this went public, and that she would need to speak to you before pursuing any investigation on her own."

"Very good Kravchenko. Tell me."

Kravchenko relays what has taken place since he spoke to the GC yesterday.

"... and when I hired a boat to take me along the coast, the captain showed me an area where rumrunners hid at one time, a deep-water crevice close to shore. When we explored the inlet, I believe we may have encountered a submarine. Would it not be wise to alert HMCS *Baffin* which I understand is the sub hunter patrolling our coast?"

At that moment, LAC Lutes knocks and enters, placing a small round tray on the table next to the ashtray. It has two mugs on it. Clark takes the one with the creamy surface.

"Thank you, Lutes. That will be all."

"Yes, Sir."

"What makes you think a submarine is lurking in our waters. It seems highly unlikely. Halifax, I could see, but around Bouctouche?"

"You yourself, Sir, mentioned how highly classified the magnetron is, and then we have dead bodies on the Air Force property. If a spy is out to get information on the magnetron or considering stealing it, wouldn't a submarine be the logical route of escape?"

His smile gone sour, Clark harrumphs at the suggestion. Kravchenko continues.

"When the boat owner, a retired fisherman named Skip, had us adrift in that cove, something forceful hit the boat from underneath, causing it to rock. We didn't see anything. While we were patrolling the coast, I approached a teacher and students with telescopes on one shore and one of the young men was stargazing the night before and saw what he thought was a reflection of glass but couldn't confirm it. This was around the same time as the signal coming from offshore somewhere in the strait. An escape route!"

Clark is tamping down fresh tobacco in his pipe as he looks at Kravchenko.

"Did this... Skip, say it could've been a big fish, maybe a dolphin or a seal, a whale maybe?"

Kravchenko is confused by the GC's attitude and his reluctance to act swiftly, but then he understands the need for accuracy before calling a ship off its usual patrol on a hunch.

"I think it unlikely, Kravchenko, anyone could get on the base, into the heavily guarded premises and actually steal the magnetron? And escape?"

Kravchenko realizes from the tone of Clark's voice he needs to tread carefully as the man is taking his comments as a personal affront. He knows this is a new posting for Clark who is more of an administrative sort and likely worried about his superior's reaction.

"Perhaps so, Sir, but would it not be best to take precautions?"

"I'll make that decision, Kravchenko, but I am willing to take your advice into consideration. I understand your thinking and agree we need to have action. It's best to follow up your suspicion and I'll contact the *Baffin* myself. Now tell me about Carter and this Francis woman."

The Warrant Officer explains what his meeting entailed, mentioning again her eagerness to take the investigation out of their hands. With Clark's approval, he'd like to bring her in to work together. Get closer to solving this dilemma. Carter is out of danger and recovering from the operation.

"Very well. I see no reason not to include her in the investigation, but I will not allow the mention of the magnetron. She will also be under strict orders to maintain the secrecy we insist upon. I will grant her access to the base, but you must remain in her presence at all times. I won't have her sticking her nose in the Air Force's doings in regard to the magnetron."

"But Sir..."

"Remind her of the Official Secrets Act. That's an order, Kravchenko."

"Yes, Sir. Inspector Francis is due at the gate in ten minutes and I told her I would meet her there."

"Francis is an unusual surname. Is she local?"

"I believe so, Sir. My understanding is Francis is a common name on First Nations land north of here. Would you like to meet her?"

"I don't think that is necessary. However, I will be connecting with her superiors to ascertain her abilities. Carry on Kravchenko."

Kravchenko finishes the last gulp of coffee and leaves.

33

He arrives at the gate at precisely 6:44 AM and sees her driving up. Her auto is a sparkling new Pontiac Fleetleader, which looks like she drove it out of the showroom this morning. There are no police markings. She stops by the gate where Kravchenko and the airman on guard await her. With a nod from Kravchenko, the solid wooden arm lifts and he waves her to enter. Inside the gate, he jumps in the car. Her hat is off and resting in the back seat. Her shirt is unbuttoned at the collar and exposes a graceful neck. Auburn hair falls a shade under her ears and has a forward curl. He wonders how she gets it all tucked up under her hat.

"Good morning, Dia."

"Good morning, Stefan. How are you feeling today?"

"Confused, but ready to go."

She looks at him with a raised brow over big eyes. He wants to be drawn into them.

"Do I meet the GC?"

"Not today, Dia. However, he's agreed to cooperate with you fully and you have access to anywhere on the base, except one area that is protected by the Canadian Secrecy Act. That is even beyond the GC's authorization. I can assure you that the building is well guarded. I have to accompany you anywhere while you are on base."

He can see her downcast look; she's not happy.

"I understand, but I want your word as a police officer that there is nothing I could use for my... I mean our... investigation within the building."

He raises his hand up in a mock courtroom gesture.

"I swear."

"Okay. Show me the bodies."

◻

There's activity everywhere. Trucks are delivering supplies, picking up refuse and transporting heavy equipment. Airmen are running or walking to different locations. A line is forming at the mess hall. The rumble of a Tiger Moth taking off distracts Dia for a moment as she watches it ascend from behind the hangars into a clear sky otherwise dotted with wandering puffs of cloud. The drive in at the posted speed limit of ten miles an hour gives them enough time between directions for making *get-to-know-you* talk.

"You from around here, Dia?"

"Yep, grew up in Big Cove, it's a reserve an hour's drive from here. Might take you a little longer. I drive fast."

He likes the way she laughs, almost like a chime.

"Turn right at the stop sign."

She waits for an official looking vehicle, drab brown, to go first.

"And you?"

"Oh, I grew up in Selena, Manitoba. It's approximately 270 miles northwest of Winnipeg. Almost on the Saskatchewan border. Small village, good people. Moved to Winnipeg right after high school. Always loved the idea of living in a big city."

He points to the hangar on their right. A large piece of enameled plywood has an enormous 5 upon its white background. It's hanging where it can be seen from the street and the runway.

"Number five. There's a parking lot on the left."

"How come there's nothing going on near the hangar. Only a few vehicles here."

"The hangar was cleared for ten more training aircraft coming by the end of the month. It's been used for odds and ends, nothing static until we stored the body and made it off limits. It's going to get busier here with more pilots coming from Australia in a few months. I wonder what they'll think of the snow?"

He doesn't expect an answer, laughing at his own joke and waves her to follow.

"Let's go."

They walk over to the side door that opens into the cavernous space. LAC Doucette comes to attention in full battle gear. Kravchenko returns the salute, introduces himself and okays Inspector Dia Francis as an authorized entrant. As ordered and with respect, he asks for ID. She has her badge in a leather folder with a picture and offers it to him. He checks it carefully and nods them through. Going toward the back of the hangar, they encounter another armed guard at the barrier set up twenty feet from the entrance to the rooms. He steps aside and salutes.

The ice has slowed the decomposition so the smell Kravchenko and Francis encounter is bearable. Dia scrunches her nose nonetheless. The first body is the one found in the field. It's a ghastly sight, as blue as a full moon. Dia has seen dead bodies before but the sight of this one bothers her. Like Kravchenko before her, she examines it closely, and does so with the other body and eventually with the head.

"Tell me how you found these, Stefan. Run me through it."

He gives her a detailed account from the time he was called in until they found the body buried in the field.

"What do you think was buried in the woods"?"

"I don't know for certain but I'm thinking a radio transmitter or receiver."

"Why would it be buried there?"

"Good question. Your guess is as good as mine. Maybe it was put in place before or after the base was built for a number of reasons. If it was a radio, there was a plan in place beforehand. There is supposed to be no entry into the field. There are *Private Property* and *No Trespassing* signs posted everywhere."

She looks at him with a questioning look on her face.

123

"Are we talking spies here?"

"That's what I'm thinking? This is an important installation involving our armed forces. Sabotage maybe? But with the... "

He hesitates, not sure of how much he should tell her, especially after the warning from Clark.

"Look Dia, I can get in a lot of trouble for this but there is a prototype of new direction-finding equipment being tested here in Scoudouc."

"Direction finding? What is that?"

"I'm the wrong guy to explain the technical aspects of it but basically when two receivers receive a radio signal, they can triangulate from their positions and locate the source. The new development will allow them to work in what they call microwave which can be more precise, smarter. That is how it was explained to me but regardless of how it works, its relevance is highly classified and important to the war effort."

"Well, it's too complicated for me but let's get back to the bodies. Why do think they've been beheaded? Any ideas, and why is there only one head?"

"I have no idea. Possibly the killer is a sadist, someone who enjoys this kind of work."

The idea makes her flesh crawl.

"And you say the uniform was clean and likely put on the first body after the dismemberment."

"I assume so. There was no blood on it and we found a spot in the woods where the butchering took place."

"And you never found the other head?"

"No, we looked but nothing."

"I noticed the head is from the second body. The shape of the cut is the same, and the location of the Adam's apple give it away. It's all very confusing. From what you have been telling me, there is more to this investigation than dead bodies. Maybe that's the reason for the bodies and heads. To throw us off."

"Possibly, but this brings tighter security. More officials, more guns. I think something is coming down too. No idea what but the direction finder is the only thing which makes sense."

"Well, I think we need to identify the bodies. It's important. What have you done in the way of identification?"

He explains Sergeant Booth's work in locating missing servicemen or people working on bases that came to a dead end. Then he explains what Carter was doing before he got shot. She checks her watch.

"Carter should be awake by now. I think we need to talk to him. I also think the bodies need to be examined by a medical examiner."

"I agree but can they come here, rather than remove the bodies? The less people involved the better."

"I can't answer that. I'll put in a call to my commanding officer and see what we can arrange. We need to use your lead on the auto as well."

"Agreed. Let's head over to the infirmary and talk to Carter."

34

Oberstleutnant Schmitz has been at his desk since five o'clock this morning. He dreads reporting the bad news to *Oberst* Meyer who he is meeting at one o'clock sharp. Ten minutes ago, his subordinate, Müller, delivered the latest report, now lying on his desk before him. He made two copies. Schmitz is still shaken up over the dressing-down he gave Müller. Although he has the authority to bump the man to the *Wehrmacht*, he uses it only as a whip and lets the threat be a motivator. He subscribes to the old adage - dreck runs downhill. He knows it is not Muller's fault, things can happen out of his control.

Meyer on the other hand expects only positive results and dishes out punishment ruthlessly. He's the world's oldest spoiled brat. His rise in the *Abwehr* can not only be attributed to his family's wealth and connections but also to his taste for violence, the more gruesome, the more enjoyable. The word *Juden* anywhere in his whereabouts is strictly forbidden. He commands that they only be referred to as *Ungeziefer* (Vermin).

Unterseeboot 498 was due to report no later than nine today with confirmation of rendezvous with package. The pickup was scheduled for midnight local time. Eastern Canada is five hours behind us so 498 would've been at sea for three hours after the connection, in open water and clear enough to send a coded confirmation signal. It is two hours and twenty minutes late. There exists a hundred reasons why but

Meyer's belligerent attitude frightens him.

He stands and runs his hand across his scalp. His nerves are shot, he needs a drink and doesn't give a damn it's so early in the day. Moving to a side cabinet he pours himself a good measure of cognac seized from distilleries in occupied France. He downs the fiery liquid in one gulp. The high alcohol content causes him to shiver before a warm glow flows up from his stomach, fusing with his brain. He proceeds to the small washroom off his office and checks his appearance in the mirror. He brushes lint off his shoulder, straightens his tie and rinses his mouth with cold water.

Back at his desk, he pops a mint in his mouth, picks up the report, looks around the office as if he will never return, and leaves. The walk up one level and down a long hallway to Meyer's office feels like his last, as if an executioner awaits his arrival.

35

8:43 am

When Kravchenko and Inspector Francis enter Clark's hospital room, they find him propped up with several pillows and a tray on a wheeled dolly before him. A fresh bandage adorns his cheek. On the tray is a half-eaten bowl of porridge, discarded peel from an orange and an empty glass. He's holding a cup in one hand blowing softly on the surface and smiles when the two visitors walk in. His gown is open over his left shoulder to expose heavy bandages. Seeing one of the visitors is a lady, modesty makes him set the cup on the tray and arrange his gown to cover his chest.

"Good morning, Sir."

Kravchenko is relieved to see Carter sitting up and in good spirits.

"Good morning to you too, Carter. This is Inspector Dia Francis with the RCMP. She will be working with me."

Carter is smitten by the Inspector. His cheeks redden when he looks in her eyes, his adoration obvious.

"Good... good morning, Inspector. Pleased to meet you."

There's an uncomfortable looking metal chair by the window. Kravchenko and Dia ignore it and stand at the foot of the bed."

"How you feeling, Carter?'

"I still have some pain in my chest. Gotta be careful not to move too much. But the pills they give me work good."

"You feeling up to telling us what happened?"

"Un huh, sure."

Carter takes them from the time he pulled over to help someone he thought lost to the gun in his gut and the slash across his face. Seven stitches to close it. The kick in his nuts (pardon his language). Forced into the woods, what the man wanted to know and his attack. The pain of the bullet, falling and then nothing else.

They're quiet for a moment. Carter stares at the floor, thinking how lucky he is. And looks up when Kravchenko passes the notebook to him.

"I noticed the last entries. Are they relevant?"

With the note pad on his thigh, Carter flips through the pages with his good arm.

"It might not be anything but when I was at the general store yesterday, the lady I spoke to mentioned one of the employees was late for work. The reason I wrote his name down is because she mentioned he was never late. I had intended to follow up to see if he made it to work, but…"

He nods to his damaged chest.

"The person's name is Tim Grant. Not sure if it will lead anywhere. Another good lead I got was from a man at a restaurant in Cocagne about a woman looking for a missing brother. The man's name is… "

He gives a quick glance at the notebook but the movement disturbs his wound and he settles back on the pillows.

"Ah… that hurts. Anyway, the guy's name is Jacques Monroe. He didn't know her name but he gave me her description. Here."

He holds the book out to Kravchenko who takes it and stands closer to Francis so she can read it too. Carter has a neat script and the small letters are easy to read.

Dirty blonde hair, ponytail. Thinks the eyes were greenish brown (hazel?). A mole on her right cheek. A little over five feet tall and as slim as a shovel handle. Maybe in her early forties.

Kravchenko lifts one brow.

"A shovel handle?"

"His words, not mine. Guess she must be a skinny gal."

Dia steps closer to the bed and offers Clark a sympathetic smile. She likes the lad. The silly grin makes his otherwise plain face amiable.

"What can you tell us about the shooter. Did you get a good look at him?"

"Sure did. He's about my height, wide shoulders, heavyset and he looked tough. Probably outweighs me by about thirty or forty pounds. Maybe in his late forties, early fifties. His eyes were light grey and cold. His nose was flat and wide. Real pale skin, like he'd never been in the sun. I'd sure know him again if I ever see him."

Kravchenko is writing this all down, as well as the description of the woman in Cocagne. He catches Dia's glance with a half-smile he's coming to realize is one of self-satisfaction. She likes what she's hearing, and so does he.

"This is good work, Carter. What was he wearing?"

Carter rubs his chin, tapping one finger while he thinks.

"Dumb as it sounds, I don't remember much about what he was wearing, paying more attention to his face and almost shi…, uh being scared of the gun and those mean looking eyes. But I remember the hat. One like Henry Fonda wore in the Grapes of Wrath, all floppy like with a peak."

Dia smiles as she recalls the movie which she saw last year on a getaway night with the girls.

"I saw that movie too. It's a newsboy hat."

"Yeah, a newsboy. And an ugly face is all I remember."

Carter laughs at his joke, wincing because it hurts. Dia laughs along and Kravchenko likes the kid's spirit.

"Any more questions, Dia?"

"What was he driving?"

"An older Dodge, not sure of the exact year but it looked like the one you told me about, Sir, grey with black running boards, only this one is blue and black. Terrible paint job. Looked like it was done with a brush. Bet it was the one bought under that Coleman fellow's name."

"What makes you say that?"

He looks to Kravchenko.

"There was a dent on the rear fender."

Dia stares back at Kravchenko.

"Does this fit?"

"Sure does. One more thing we can track down. Did you have a chance to have the heel prints enlarged?"

"Yes, Sir. I left them with the guard inside the conference room in Hangar 5. I was sure you'd find them there if I didn't get a chance to leave them for you later."

"Thank you, Aircraftsman 2 Jeremy Carter."

He bends and whispers in Carter's ear.

"Start thinking of yourself as Leading Aircraftsman Jeremy Carter. I'll make sure it happens."

Kravchenko backs off and with a wink and a salute, leads Dia out of the room. Carter lies his head back, closes his eyes and thinks of the raise in pay. After imagining all the ways to spend it, he lulls himself to sleep thinking about the inspector's pretty face.

◻

Outside the closed door and halfway to the front of the building, they meet Sergeant Booth who tells them he is on his way to see Carter. After introductions, he apologizes for not coming earlier but his regular duties required his attention. He has a large manila envelope under one arm.

"This is for you, Sir. Information I could gather on the missing man in Amherst. Having a look at it myself, I don't think it is either of our... guests? But that's only my opinion, Sir."

"Thank you, Sergeant. After your visit with Carter, can you arrange for someone to retrieve the car he borrowed and inform the owners. Then you can return to your normal duties but be ready to react should I call upon you. Please leave your whereabouts with the duty officer."

Booth salutes and doffs his hat at the inspector. Thinks she's a little on the slender side but she's cute.

Dia and Kravchenko head to the exit. They pause on the front steps and she stands with her arms akimbo and faces Kravchenko.

"I think we should deal with the woman in Cocagne and Tim Grant at the store. See where that leads us. Keeping an eye out for... what year is the car?"

"1935 Dodge."

"I'm not sure what that year looks like."

"They're squarer on the back than the new ones. Wider running boards, pot lights on the front and the spare tire on the driver's side toward the front."

"Should we split up or stay together?"

"I think we should do it together. You might catch something I miss and vice versa."

"All right then, let's go. We can use my car."

She has a thought as they walk towards her vehicle.

"I need to find a phone and make the call to my chief, get a medical examiner over here as soon as possible. I'd like to see the site where you found the bodies after that. And we should follow up on heel prints if you think it's important."

"Yeah, we should. Anything that might help."

36

Before becoming a secret agent for the motherland, Iron Spear changed professions from meat cutter to carpenter. Those same skills, and impeccable credentials, got him a job at the Scoudouc Air Force Base. This week he traded shifts like he planned, and now only has to report to work at four o'clock. Today he makes his final preparations for the strike tomorrow evening.

Sitting in a workshop attached to the house he lives in, he is modelling a vacuum jar similar to the one he carries every day in his lunch pail, which gets inspected at each shift, going in and coming out. He's not worried about the coming out part because the guard shifts change at the same time he knocks off work, which is midnight. It's the going in he's concerned about. If it's Peterson on duty at four, he has to be careful. The man looks closely at everything so his model must be perfect.

Earlier this morning, he filled a cannister with the plaster of Paris he mixed up. Not having a kiln, he had to let it air dry for four hours. The block sitting on the desk is a perfect cylindrical object the same height as his vacuum jar, manufactured by Stanley. Using files and carving knifes, he whittles away and files until the likeness before him is identical in shape. All he has to do now is bore a hole in the bottom slightly larger than the stick of dynamite he stole.

Once the hole is made, he sets about to paint the model the same color as his vacuum jar. Finishing up an hour later, he sets it aside for the paint to dry. Using his original vacuum jar, he removes the metal plate from the front so he can attach it to the model later. All he has to do then is insert the dynamite and seal the bottom.

The detonator and fuse will be strapped to his thigh under his coveralls. They stopped patting him down. Only the new guards he hasn't met do a cursory pat until they get to know him. There haven't been any new guards for over a month but to be sure he will wrap it tightly so there are no sharp edges. He already has a gun and another knife hidden on base.

Leaving the workshop, he locks the door and returns to the house to get ready for work. His goal tonight is to check on the building where he suspects the device he intends to steal is located. He assumed it would be near the radio rooms where all the antennae are located. The extra security confirms his suspicions. At night he has no supervisor, just a list of tasks, small repairs around the base, to be accomplished. He can easily take a detour around the building with the truck he uses.

He's already having dreams of how many more men he can kill.

37

10:22 am

Dia parks the Pontiac to the side of the general store. Glancing up at the grey clouds moving from the west, she and Kravchenko make their way to the front entrance.

"Looks like it might rain."

"Yes, hope not though. The wool on this suit gets itchy when it gets wet."

They are a pair who don't go unnoticed. Her crisp uniform and tall bearing make her look formidable in a flattering feminine way. Kravchenko in neat Air Force Blues looks official and as often as the locals are familiar with seeing airmen, he stands out with his broad shoulders and poster boy looks. Several elderly men are standing off to the side at the front with coffees and cigarettes. They go quiet as they watch the duo enter the store.

Inside the place is busy with a line up at the cash of three ladies with shopping carts. Kravchenko catches the eye of the young cashier and asks if the manager is in. She wordlessly points to a man at the end of the row facing her wearing a white knee-length lab type coat similar to what a doctor would wear. He's placing cans of soup on the shelves when the pair approaches him. Dia speaks to him with Kravchenko standing close behind.

"Excuse me Sir, are you the manager?"

A scowl on his face shows that the man is in a bad mood. He stops

135

what he's doing and looks Dia up and down with distaste either from being disturbed or because she's a woman. He's shorter than her, twice as wide. Frizzy hair surrounds a bald dome.

"Yes, I am. How can I help you?"

"We're looking for Tim Grant?"

"So am I. The sod never showed up for his shift yesterday and he's not here this morning."

Dia looks to Kravchenko with a knowing nod. He steps forward.

"When was the last time you saw him?"

"Not since Tuesday. He could've at least let us know. I know he doesn't have a phone but he could've gotten us a message. He's a good employee and even though I'm short staffed, the young girl on the cash needed some extra hours. So... now if you'll excuse me, I have work to do."

Dia doesn't like his attitude and steps close enough that he has to back off.

"I will not excuse you, Mister. We are investigating an urgent matter and you will cooperate, or if you would prefer, I can close this business down right now and haul you off to the station."

Kravchenko glares at the man, his look telling the manager they mean business and are not to be trifled with.

"All right, all right. What do you want to know?"

"What does he look like? Any distinguishing features? Any photos?"

The man describes Tim Grant and Kravchenko is writing it down when he stops suddenly, looks up at the man and interrupts him.

"What did you say about his foot?"

"I said he broke his left ankle when he was younger. Wasn't set right. Kept him out of the service. He walks fine, just has a crooked foot."

Dia looks at Kravchenko with a knowing look. She saw the corpse's ankle too. This is all they need to know.

"Thank you, Mr...?"

"Cormier, last name's Cormier."

"Now one more question, Mr. Cormier. You said he moved into an apartment. Where did he live previously?"

"With his parents. They live about a mile from here going toward Moncton. The first farmhouse on the right."

"Thank you again. If by any chance you hear anything else, please report it to the RCMP detachment in Moncton to my attention right away. Now we can let you get back to work."

She gives him one of her business cards which he pockets with a frown. He returns to stocking his shelf and doesn't watch them leave. Outside Kravchenko and Dia are smiling, not at anything amusing, but at the fact they may have an identity.

"I think we've found our man, Stefan. Let's double check with his parents. You mentioned a mole on his back."

"If this Tim Grant does have a mole on his back, how are we going to find out without telling them their son is dead?"

"I'm not sure. It's going to be a heart breaker for sure. I hate being the bearer of bad news. I think it might be best to tell them the truth and ask them for confirmation. We'll also have to tell them it will be a few days before we can release the body."

They drive to the first farm on the right. It's a small operation. A group of cows, maybe ten or so, roam the field to the right. Two horses share the pasture fenced in with cedar poles overlapped upon each other. A man is in the yard tinkering with a truck, the hood up, bent over the fender on the driver's side. A black and white collie runs toward their car barking at the intrusion. The man whistles and the dog runs back to him and sits at his feet. Both have a curious stare when Dia drives up to the end of driveway a couple of car lengths from where the man is working.

"Want to do this together?" says Kravchenko.

"I think one of us is enough. I'll approach him. There's no easy way."

Dia greets the man. Although the window is down on Kravchenko's side, their voices are muffled by the distance. He watches the farmer's rection. An affirmative shake of the head. He holds his hand up to form a small circle. Kravchenko guesses the gesture to indicate the size of the mole. After a few moments of listening to Dia, he stumbles to the side of the truck and leans against it, his head hanging. Dia approaches him and places a hand on his arm. When the farmer looks up, Kravchenko can see the tears running along the man's cheek. Dia then returns to the car. The farmer shakes his head before ambling toward the house likely to share the bad news. Dia slides back in the driver's seat.

"Poor man. It's his oldest child. Three girls and a younger brother left. I didn't go into details about the missing head. No need to trouble them right now. They have enough to handle with the grief of knowing he's dead. I explained to him that because the body was discovered on Air Force property in suspicious circumstances, it could not be released at present, but that someone will keep them posted. We would look after it to have him taken to the funeral home of their choice."

Kravchenko notices the shaded eyes and downturned mouth and can see all this troubles her.

"Not easy, is it?"

"No, and I hope I never become hardened to death or take it for granted. Right, you ready to head to Cocagne?

"Un-huh. Let's do it."

38

Kravchenko takes the lead in Cocagne as Dia is still troubled by the look in the farmer's eyes when she told him about his son. Telling her he'll be right back, he enters the first restaurant in Cocagne. There are only two. This one is at the foot of the wooden bridge which joins the two sections of the community which are situated across the narrowest part of the Cocagne River where it flows out into the bay. He hustles in as there is a drizzle in the air. He likes the look of the village. People smile at him even though they don't know him. Maybe it's the uniform, maybe they're just nice folks.

Stepping inside the premises, he sees seats along the front windows, several in the center and a counter with stools on the back wall. About a dozen patrons are scattered throughout the dining area with a group of four elderly men in the corner to his left. A low hum of conversation greets him amid the rattling of pots and pans from the kitchen to the right. The aroma of frying meat and boiling vegetables wafts from the open doors. A waitress is near the cash register bent over an order pad. She looks up when Kravchenko approaches. Her hair pulled back in a severe bun but there's a twinkle in her eyes and a natural smile.

"How can I help you today, flyboy?"

Kravchenko is impressed she recognizes his Air Force uniform. He always gets called a soldier although he really doesn't mind.

"I'm looking for a gentleman by the name of Jacques Monroe."

"It's your lucky day, my friend. Jacques a regular. That's him in the corner with his coffee buddies. The gent with the grey beard. Can I get you something?"

He takes a quick look up at a menu printed on the wall behind her.

"Yes, please. Two of your ham and cheese sandwiches, one with no lettuce and two coffees to go, one black and one with two sugars. Thanks. I'll pick them up in a minute after I speak to Mr. Monroe."

"Gotcha."

Kravchenko steps toward the table of four men. The conversation stops as he nears them. A man in uniform is a curious sight in the small village. The man with the beard is sitting facing him on the left side of the table. Kravchenko doesn't want to alarm them so he wears a big smile.

"Mr. Monroe?"

"Mr. Monroe is my father. Call me Jack. How can I help ya, Soldier?"

Through the large window, Kravchenko points to Dia in the car outside in the front parking lot.

"I'm working with an officer of the RCMP, who you can see is waiting in the car. We're trying to track down a local fellow. One of my men was speaking to you yesterday about a woman who came in looking for a missing person on Saturday. You remember that?"

It takes the man a moment to recall the incident.

"Was he in uniform?"

"Nope, dressed casually."

"Hmmm, yeah, a young lad. I remember now but like I told him, I don't know her name. I gave him a description. She didn't seem too upset or worried. She comes here sometimes. Hang on."

The man waves to the other waitress serving a couple two tables away. He speaks to her in French.

"Hey Doris, *venez ici pour une minute.*"

He looks to Kravchenko and seeing the puzzled look on his face, realizes the man doesn't understand and switches back to English. The waitress, with big eyes and a ponytail, is chewing gum like her life depended on it.

"You remember the lady who was in here Saturday looking for her brother. The skinny gal. I've seen her around but don't know her name, and I remember you were chatting to her."

"*Ah oui*, Lucille Gallant."

Kravchenko gets her attention.

"Do you know where I could find her?"

"She works at the fish plant by the church. With the lobster season, it is open seven days a week. Just up the shore road toward Bouctouche, not far. When you step outside and look toward the island, you'll see the church steeple. She might be there today if it's not her day off. They usually break for lunch at 12:30.

"Thank you, ma'am. And thank you, Mr... Jack."

Both nod and carry on while Kravchenko goes back to the counter where his sandwiches and coffee are ready.

"That'll be $3.20, please."

Kravchenko tips his head back at the table with the four men.

"How much for the bill at that table?"

"Give me a minute."

She flips a few pages over on her writing pad, removes the pencil from behind her ear and tallies up the amount.

"They were all big eaters today. Each had the breakfast special. It's $7.40 altogether."

Kravchenko does a quick calculation, removes a twenty-dollar bill from his wallet and passes it to her.

"Divide the change up between you and the other waitress."

Her eyes go wide. It's a considerable tip.

"Well, *merci*, flyboy. Very kind of you."

Kravchenko leaves with his package and gets back in the car. Noticing the clear sky in the south, he's relieved the drizzle has let up.

"I brought you a coffee and a sandwich. Hope you like ham and cheese."

She smiles warmly at his thoughtfulness.

"I do, thank you. How did you make out? I saw you talking to those men at the table."

"The lady's name is Lucille, and she works just up the road toward the church. The plant runs all week with the lobster season open. So she should be there today. The waitress says they break for lunch in a half hour. Let's go wait in the church parking lot, eat our sandwiches and then we can go see her."

"Good idea. I didn't realize how hungry I was."

◻

She parks the car near the church where they can see the two brick buildings of the plant next to a busy wharf. They put the windows down, breath in the salty air coming off the bay. The breeze changes directions occasionally like it's not sure where it wants to go and sometimes they get a whiff of fish offal from the plant, but it doesn't hang around. During their impromptu lunch, they talk about the case and Kravchenko is charmed by Dia's intelligence and attention to detail. After the sandwiches are gone and they are both sipping on their hot beverages, he checks out her left hand holding the paper cup and sees there is no wedding band or engagement ring.

"You have a boyfriend, Dia?"

She looks at him with a frown.

"Is that question relevant to our investigation, Warrant Officer?"

He blushes and looks off past the church to the manse and the bay so she can't see his face.

"No, no it's not. Just curious. Most women I meet these days are married or engaged, with many of their men off to war."

"I did have a boyfriend up until this spring when I caught the bugger with my roommate, both *in flagrant delicto*, in my shared apartment. I returned early from a week in Fredericton where I was working with several officers on a murder case on the Saint Mary's reserve near there. I kicked both of them out. How about you? I don't see any wedding band."

"No, me neither. Probably around the same time as you, I received a letter from my former girlfriend who is stationed in England with the Medical Corp. A goodbye letter actually. She found someone else. Since then, I've been too busy for romance I'm afraid."

"Hunh. I know what that's like."

They're both feeling awkward from the conversation and the underlying attraction. Kravchenko changes the subject.

"You want to take the lead on this? Woman to woman. Might be easier."

"Yeah, good idea. I'll deal with her supervisor if we have to. You're not in an official position to be questioning her anyway."

"Right. I'll wait here"

Dia checks her watch and sees it's almost time for the lunch break and it's confirmed by a short toot on an air whistle. Within minutes they see a group of people leaving the building, some heading to vehicles parked off to the side. Four women come out as a group, all holding lunch pails, one of them carrying what looks like a towel. They proceed to one of the picnic tables off to the side. The one with the cloth wipes the moisture away. When they plunk into the seats, two aside, the sun breaks through the stringy clouds and their smiles turn as bright as the yellow rays. Lucille Gallant is easy to spot from the description Clark wrote down. She's the shortest of the bunch and has the lightest hair. Dia proceeds to where they sit. Kravchenko watches.

The woman all look up at Dia, and she directs her conversation to the most petite of the group. Kravchenko sees the woman nodding and Dia pointing to him. The lady leaves her unopened lunch box on the table and follows Dia back to the car. He gets out and meets them at the front. Dia points to him

"This is Warrant Officer Stefan Kravchenko of the Air Force Service Police. Stefan, this is Lucille Gallant."

Allan Hudson

"Hello Miss Gallant."

Her voice is as small as she is, and he has to bend slightly to catch what she says.

"It's Mrs. Gallant actually, but please call me Lucy."

He has to be careful. Not knowing for sure if the other body is her brother, he doesn't want to cause her unnecessary grief. He shades the truth slightly when he speaks to her.

"All right, Lucy it is. The reason we want to talk to you is that you were looking for someone a few days ago. A young man had an accident on base, and he's lost his memory and has no ID. Have you located your brother?"

She places her folded hands over her chest and stares back at him with a stunned look.

"Oh, my goodness, I hope it's not him. It can't be. He wouldn't go on the base. Normally I don't worry too much about Pierre when he ventures off. He's done it before. He likes to use his uncle's cabin in Scoudouc sometimes or to camp in the woods. When he left on one of his camping trips on Saturday, he said he'd be back on Tuesday or Wednesday. I was just asking around in case he needed a drive. He usually hitches rides with folks. I don't think he'd want to miss our sister's birthday dinner tonight. I still ain't too worried. He'll likely show up today."

Kravchenko sees the doubt when he looks at her closely. Although her eyes are somewhat hopeful, her close-lipped smile is forced.

"Well, we certainly hope he does. How old is he?"

Brighter now, they can see how much she likes talking about her brother.

"He's the baby. He'll be eighteen in another month, day after mine, although we're six years apart. Says he's gonna join up and learn to fly. One of his older friends is stationed at Scoudouc. A uniform like yours... Sir."

Kravchenko smiles at her use of sir, but he is really thinking her brother might be too young for the cadaver they found in the field. The medical examiner will tell them more.

"Call me Stefan. So, four days camping is not unusual?"

With a shake of her head and a wave of her slender hand, she chuckles at his question.

"He's been gone seven or eight days before. He's like our father, a real outdoorsman. They're happier in the forest. They fish and hunt and know what kind of stuff they can eat, including bugs."

She shakes her shoulders and makes a contorted face.

"Yuk! I can't think of anything worse. No rough camping for me."

"Can you tell us what he looks like?"

"His hair is darker than mine, browner. Short on top, brown eyes, average face, a thin nose and beautiful eyebrows. Me and my sister are jealous. Nothing unusual. But..."

She pauses for second, a memory smoothing her forehead.

"Thinking of his eyebrow, I remember the time he was only five and trying to get away from our dog who wanted a part of his cookie. Pierre tripped on a rug and hit his head on the seat of a rocking chair. It made a small cut through the eyebrow. You can't notice it but if you look closely, there is a narrow slit where the tiny hairs never grow."

"Anything else we should look for?"

"Nothing comes to mind. He didn't have any other scars. Maybe his birthmark, a tiny red mark in the crook of the knee at the back. Very small."

Kravchenko can't remember seeing any such mark on the cadavers. Maybe he didn't look close enough.

"Thank you, Lucy. I need you to keep this information quiet due to the Wartime Secrecy Act because it happened on the base. If I have any more news, we'll contact you."

"Now you have me worried. Can you please let me know?"

Dia steps closer and puts her hand on Lucy's shoulder, not wanting the woman to worry at this point because they don't know for sure.

"We will, Lucy, and thanks for answering our questions. We took up most of your lunch hour."

"What am I going to tell my friends at the table?"

"Tell them we are with the enlistment office and that your brother contacted us and we're looking for him."

She considers the idea with closed mouth scrutiny.

"Ok, sounds real. My neighbour has a phone and the number is 180, ring 33."

Kravchenko writes it down. He and Dia say goodbye. Lucy returns to the table of curious women. Dia gets in the car and looks to Kravchenko.

"Wartime Secrecy Act?"

He shrugs and smiles.

"I had to think of something and actually it does exist. It wouldn't be applicable in this case but she doesn't know that."

Dia puts the car in reverse and grins at her partner.

"We have work to do my friend."

"We do. Let's go back and look at the body again."

"I also want to see where the bodies were found, and we need to find the second head."

39

2:10 pm

Kravchenko directs Dia to turn left before the gate into the base. They cross the bridge and stop where Carter and Kravchenko walked up the stream on the side opposite the base. Leaving the automobile, he takes her down into the abandoned field, points out the road and waves his arm across the expanse of the field.

"This is all expropriated land owned by the Department of National Defence and signs for no trespassing are posted everywhere. The fields lie fallow now. We can follow the river and I'll show you the spot where something was dug up, the killing area and then the grave further down the field. The first body was found on the other side."

He stops and points through some brush where Carter found the first body.

"We can have another look later."

They carry on until they are at the tramped down grass where Kravchenko runs his imagined scenario to her. He leads her around the huge tree marking the spot and points out the hole. He then shows her the gap in the trees where the killing field is. He remains standing off to the side as Dia bends to inspect the hole and the surrounding terrain. The earlier rain has left the ground damp. The leaves of the trees drip with moisture if rubbed against. She looks back at Kravchenko.

"There are fresh footprints here. Made this morning."

Kravchenko bends to where she is pointing. He sees the boot

prints, two of them in the soft dirt, the heel pronounced. He rubs his chin as he thinks.

"The heel mark looks familiar. Maybe I'm imagining it, but I get a weird feeling from this. We need to look at the enlargements Carter had made. Wish I had a camera."

Dia steps back carefully and goes to the edge of the forest. She shades her eyes from the sun, looks around the field as if someone is watching them and then focuses on the buildings she can see on the base.

"Didn't you say this area is off limits?"

"Yes."

"There shouldn't be any other footprints. We have no way of knowing where these might have come from but it tells us that someone was here today. Could the killer have returned, and why?"

"It might've been anybody. I was told people still sneak on the land to fish. I did find a fishing creel and rod, like I mentioned last night."

"Is it far from here to where the enlargements are, Stefan? Could you go get them while I sniff around some more. I'll be careful."

"Okay. I'll be about ten or fifteen minutes."

He leaves and walks back to where he can cross the stream without getting soaked. Dia treads carefully around the hole and steps toward the pool of hardened blood. She gasps when she enters the cleared area and sees the large stain. Inspecting everything closely, she sees older tracks and surmises they belong to Kravchenko or the killer. It makes her wonder about the fresh footprints, and she goes back to where she saw them. Studying the ground closely, she can see indents in the leaves and debris where the track looks fresh. They veer off to the left through a thicket of small bushes and circumnavigate the whole area.

She continues to follow the rough trail. Broken branches leave a tale of recent passing, some of the snapped twigs look recent. Although she wouldn't know, the footsteps go beyond the spot where Kravchenko found the pile of clothing, fishing rod and creel. She enters a small clearing and stops short at what she sees. A canvas bag, like a haversack with shoulder straps, the size of an average suitcase, is bundled up on one side of the clearing under overhanging branches of spruce trees. All around is debris which she guesses came from the bag. It includes a canteen, a small bottle with wooden matches inside, an unfurled sleeping bag, rope, an unopened can of beans and another of spam. Two pieces of fabric are caught on tree branches to the side. They look like lightweight canvas or cotton duck fabric. Dia guesses it could be part of a pup tent. Ants are crawling over dried pieces of what looks like jerky littered on the ground. The whole area could be a camp site. The ground, a circle of maybe twenty feet, is hard packed in spots, uneven with some dips filled with moss in the shadows or dead leaves in the others. She steps back and, in a flash, remembers Lucy telling of her brother going off into the woods. Maybe this is where he used to come to. Then she notices the path.

Checking the sun over her right shoulder to orient herself, she eases around the campsite to the edge of the path and surmises that it runs toward the base. The southern leg is older, evidenced by the greyness of the broken limbs and the ground worn bare in spots. The opposite direction looks newer with brush freshly hacked and pushed to the side. They've not even lost their needles yet. The trail can be measured in months instead of years. Dia is itching to follow the trail toward the base but knows she needs to wait for Stefan. She pauses and removes her hat, wiping perspiration from her brow. Turning back toward the campsite she faces the way she came in. She stands with her fists on her hips, stares at the mess and thinks Kravchenko should soon be here.

Not soon enough.

40

Iron Spear was vetted by the Dept. of Defense. His past was so cleverly created by the *Abwehr* that it survived all inquiries. He works in maintenance and he has to be at work at four o'clock. Presently he's sitting at his kitchen table with an eight by ten aerial photo of the Air Force base in front of him. A building near the back edge of the property has a red X near it. Another building almost directly in front has two XX's near it. The third last building up the street has a circle around it. The large hangars are to the left and one in the middle has a ? and a 5 on the roof in the photo. A red line follows the main road in from the main highway to the parking lot near the bottom right of the photo past the hangars.

He goes over his plan once more of what he needs to do tonight. The maintenance shed he works out of is circled. Double X is where the heavy guard is. X is where he strikes. He needs to check his timing, walking between buildings, allowing for possible interruptions. He has to know what tasks are scheduled for tomorrow night's shift and he needs an excuse and permission to park his car in the truck pool then. For his own ease of mind, he wants to double check that his weapons are still secure.

He's quite sure LAC Noseworthy, the young man from Newfoundland, is on the gate tonight so there will be no pat down. He hopes the kid's not on duty tomorrow night. He likes him and he's not a Jew. Iron Spear is taking the fuse and blasting caps in tonight. He knows where he'll hide them. He's working in the building with the electrician and a helper tonight. He slides the photo aside and sits back for a minute before he has to leave for work. He thinks of his homeland from which he's been gone for three years. He thinks of his family, the torturous years of trying to overcome his grief. He shudders remembering the ruin and poverty after the first conflict, and the struggle through the subsequent Depression which claimed his wife and two boys through malnutrition and disease.

His mind swirls with thoughts of revenge and the New Reich.

41

Dia is about to walk forward to inspect the haversack on the ground when she is startled by the snapping of a branch directly behind her. Her immediate response is to crouch but it's too late. She is struck on the back of her head with a heavy object. Her movement lessens the impact, otherwise it may have killed her. Her hat flies off and the blow propels her forward to the ground, face in the twigs, arms and legs sprawled out, unconscious.

The man standing behind her stares at the inert body with a sadistic grin. As he drops a broken branch the size of a baseball bat, he can see that she is still breathing. Tiny yellow blossoms near her mouth move when she exhales. How pretty! But he has to finish her off. One more day is all he needs. He regrets having to kill her and he can't use his gun, too close to the base. He has only a jackknife but it's sharp enough for the task. Stepping over her back, one foot on each side, he proceeds to reach down and grab her by the hair. He's stunned when a voice calls out and footsteps crunch the undergrowth coming closer. Panic grips him inside. He thought she was alone.

"Dia, where are you?"

His pulse quickens. He can't get caught. He runs back to the base.

Kravchenko is alerted to racing feet stomping and snapping broken twigs and branches. A yell of pain propels him forward. He drops the envelope with the photos and runs past the killing floor, through a

152

tangle of scrub brush, around a stand of young poplar and older trees to break out into the camp site. The sound of running feet to the right in the direction of the base is dying off. He starts to run, side stepping the items scattered about and spies Dia sprawled on forest floor close to the perimeter of the clearing, her face on the ground.

Rushing to her side he kneels and checks her neck for a pulse, alarmed by the spot of blood on her scalp. A gush of relief runs through him when he feels her heart beating. He looks over to the trail and knows he should be after whoever did this. But more important is the need to get her to the infirmary. Bending to take her head, a delicate silhouette among tiny flowers on the moss, causes him pause. It's a dumb thought to have at that moment but he can't help himself. She is beautiful. He turns her head enough to straighten her neck. He can feel her steady breath on his hand. He notices that the area of blood on her scalp is small and already gelled in her hair. He checks that she's not bleeding anywhere else. Grabbing the sleeping bag, and shaking the debris off of it, he rolls it into a padded pillow and places it beside her head, then turns her over with her head tipped so she is not lying on the wound. With a grip on her arm and shoulder he urges her body onto its back. The motion causes her to stir.

With eyes closed, a soft groan escapes her lips and her hand goes to the wound.

"Ahh, that stings."

"Lie still, Dia. You've taken a blow to the head. It's stopped bleeding though."

She blinks a dozen times and opens her eyes. She is lying under the overhanging branches of a tall spruce. Her head hurts and spins until she focuses on Kravchenko's face an arm's length away. Any other time she might consider his devastating, now it is a welcome sight. She winces as she tries to sit up.

"Maybe you should rest, Dia."

"Never mind rest. Help me sit up... please."

He gets a grip under her shoulders. Their faces are inches apart.

Her heart takes a gallop. He's blushing from her proximity but lifts her up enough so that she can sit with her legs straightened out. Then he helps her shimmy back a few feet until she can rest against a large tree. He pushes his hat back off his forehead and stands back with his arms akimbo.

"We need to get you to the infirmary. Have that bump looked at."

"Just give me a minute. I'm okay, and you say it's not bleeding. Wish I had an aspirin or two, maybe ten."

With a halfhearted smile, she touches the bump growing on the back of her head and winces. When she tries to straighten her hair, the icky presence of drying blood smears her finger. She wipes the dead leaves off her uniform jacket and trousers. Kravchenko retrieves her hat and passes it to her.

"What if I ordered you to go to the infirmary?"

"Hunh. You can order all you like but I'm not under your command, Sir. In fact, I could order you to not bring up the subject again. Need I remind you, I'm in charge of this investigation."

He plays along with her.

"Not on the base or National Defense property. I'm in charge of the investigation."

Their mock frowns turn into laughter, and she tells him to stop.

"It hurts when I laugh. Oh gosh. It makes me feel better though. My momma always said laughter is the best medicine. Give me a hand, Sir."

She extends her hand to grab on to his and pull herself up. His strong grip is reassuring. Almost to her feet, and feeling dizzy, she slips on a cluster of leaves and falls into his arms. He has to balance himself from the unexpected weight so that they both don't fall so he grips her to his chest with strong arms while keeping a solid stance, feet braced. Their faces are inches apart. He gets lost in the pool of her eyes and she melts in the comfort of his arms. As if it is the most natural thing in the world, he kisses her. She resists at first but then gives in to the softness of his lips, her heart thudding. She pulls away, shaking her head, loosening herself from his embrace.

"I'm sorry, Stefan. This is not a good time."

His cheeks ripen and he feels awkward.

"I'm sorry too, Dia. I don't know what came over me. I apologize for being so forward."

She touches him on the forearm and squeezes gently.

"I know what came over you, Stefan. It came over me too. I like you. When this is over, maybe we can get to know each other better. However, I don't think we should let our personal feelings get in the way of our investigation."

"Yes, you're right."

He shuffles his feet and looks around the camp site. Both of them feel shy.

"How's the head?"

"The aching is slowing down. Still hurts. I feel a bit woozy but I'm good."

He's not sure if he believes her. Her eyes are clear but she looks a bit disoriented. He sweeps his hand around the mess and changes the subject.

"What do we have here, Dia?"

"I think this is where Lucy's brother camped. If we discover that the second body is him, it might explain what he was doing in the area. Maybe he discovered something he shouldn't have. Maybe both bodies are simply a result of being in the wrong place at the wrong time. I think the hole where something was buried is what started all this. Let's do a quick search here and then I think we should follow the path back toward the base and see if we can find any clues of who hit me. Then we look at the body again."

"Whoever accosted you is long gone now. But yes, it's a good plan."

He remembers something.

"I'd forgotten about this, but I heard a yell. Not a yell really but a surprised shout. Don't know if it means anything."

"It might've been me."

"No, this was after I called out your name. There was a running away noise, then the yell, and more running. I followed the sound through the woods and found you. Maybe he hurt himself. Let's hurry. There's not a lot to see here. Oh wait, I dropped the envelope with the photos. Let me go get it first."

She puts her hat on, pulling the peak more forward so that the back rests above the wound. They rifle through the debris, examining the haversack last. Dia walks over and unfurls the canvas bag. When the top flaps open a terrific stink assails her and she thinks of rotted fruit. She jolts back and retches at her feet. Kravchenko was untangling the flaps of canvas from the trees when he hears her vomiting. He drops the cloth and runs to her, thinking her wound is making her ill.

"What is it, Dia? What's wrong?"

She has her back to him, bent over, wiping the spittle from her lips, and waves him away.

"It's from the stink in that bag. I think there might be rotten apples or oranges. It's awful."

He smiles at her forlorn look. Rubbing his chin, he indicates there is something on hers. Another wipe and she forces a smile.

"I'm fine, Stefan, stop looking at me like that."

"Okay. Just take it easy. Let's see what's in there."

He snaps off a dead limb the length of a yardstick from one of the trees. Poking at the bag, he digs in the lips of the unzipped opening, holding his nose with one hand in preparation for the coming odour. With the other hand, he uses the branch to lift the top flap. A dozen flies rush from the opening. Dia is standing a foot behind him where she can see. Both of them gasp out loud. They've found the other head.

42

Blood drips from the gash on his calf. He stumbled in a dip in the ground and fell against a large tree with the bottom branches hacked off to clear the path. His leg rammed into a pointed dead branch sticking out of the tree, the end of which tapered like a knife. It tore the bottom of his uniform and stuck in his calf muscle. The forward motion of him falling opened the wound. Yelping in pain, he jerks his leg away from the pointed wood, ripping a piece of fabric from his uniform.

His fear of getting caught is greater than the pain of the cut. He keeps running. He needs to get back to his car. After ten minutes he is at the terminus of the trail. It stops at the edge of a field, behind Hangar Number 8, the last one at the west side of the base. The field is overgrown from not being tended for a long time. Young growth of poplar and birch trees grow random and wild, most tall enough to hide a man. They provide a cover to the fence that runs from the edge of the forest to the front of the hangar.

He stumbles to the back of the huge building and makes his way to the eastern wall where the civilian workers park their vehicles. Official vehicles and Air Force personnel park along the fence. He stops at the far corner and peers round the edge to see if the way is clear to his own car. He has to wait for two civilians who are getting into an older Dodge truck. When they leave, he hustles to his own auto, a 1940 Chevrolet, black, like all autos owned by the Air Force. He has to go home and fix the cut on his leg.

No one is expecting him at the office. He left an hour ago for a late dentist appointment, telling the duty officer he would return in the morning at his usual time. He gets in position to drive away and sucks in his breath through clenched teeth, trying to ignore the pain. He can feel the blood running down his leg. He has his head down, his hat tipped forward to keep his face in shadow and drives slowly so as not to attract attention. Luckily he sees no one he recognizes. He slams the steering wheel with a clenched fist, angry at the woman police officer. He was only supposed to get in and get out, a quick jaunt to get rid of the evidence. The warrant officer is getting too close for his comfort. And now with the bothersome police it's even worse. Checking his watch, he calculates how much longer he needs to wait before he meets Iron Spear. Tonight, at one hundred hours. Another nine hours. He's not looking forward to it.

43

4:12 pm

Just short of a hundred feet into the path, Kravchenko discovers the reason he heard someone shout out. A tall fir tree borders the edge of the path. Limbs have been chopped off and one of them about a foot off the ground is sticking out from the bole of the tree. Why he noticed it is because of the light blue wool fabric, a shredded piece the size of a playing card, still attached to it. He stops short of the tree and gets Dia's attention.

"Look there. There's the reason someone called out. Looks like he caught his leg on that sharp branch."

They both crouch down and Dia lifts the fabric away from the pointed end.

"Ooh. There's a piece of skin on it and some blood. I'm not touching that. What do you make of the cloth, Stefan?"

He holds it up so he can see it better. The tall trees blot out the sun and the deep shadows clog the forest. Recognizing the fabric and texture, he holds the torn cloth next to his thigh and looks at Dia. The material is the same as his uniform trousers.

"Damn! A member of the Air Force. Not good. What could they possibly be doing at the camp site? It had to be intentional. No one would venture this far off base. There would be no reason for a serviceman to be here. This is strange."

"It could be the killer, Stefan. He would have access to uniforms and the land behind the hangars. It wouldn't be odd for someone to be on the property if they were stationed here."

"It's possible. Let's follow the trail and see where it comes out."

He tucks the remnant in his jacket pocket and leads them on. They are looking side to side, watching for any unusual movement or a possible ambush. At the edge of the forest, they stop where the hacked-out trail ends at the hem of the field. Dia points to the tracks in front of them in the tall grass.

"This is where they went toward the hangar. C'mon."

She leads the way through the field, twisting around the errant growth to get to the edge of the large building. She points to the fence.

"Not much in the way of security at this end of the base, Stefan."

"With the dense forest they likely thought there was no need. There's only vacant land surrounding the base. There are signs everywhere to keep out or to stay away. The whole village and surrounding population have been more than cooperative. We are not anywhere near a war zone."

"I guess the planners didn't consider spies."

"Guess not. The base isn't necessarily a place for sabotage although the work here is valuable to the war effort. It's too big for any one person to do any major harm."

"I agree, but what about the big secret?"

He shrugs and shakes his head.

"I don't know, Dia. Are they after the magnetron, and the bodies are there to throw us off, make us look in the wrong direction? Or is there a psychopath posing as a service man? There are over three hundred personnel on base. It could be anyone."

He gestures with a tip of his head.

"I see the tracks follow the back of the hangar to the parking lot. Maybe someone saw something. Let's go check."

When they move past the back wall of the hangar, a half dozen civilians and an officer are returning to their cars. Dia and Stefan watch the activity. He points to the group heading toward them.

160

"Shift change, Dia. The people milling about likely didn't see anything, but you take the left and I'll take the right. We'll ask if anyone saw anyone coming out the way we just did."

They move about the vehicles, asking the same question but get head shakes and denials. No one saw anything. They meet at the opposite end of the lot. Frustration sits on both of their chins. Kravchenko leans back against the fender of another Chevrolet and crosses his arm.

"You discover anything, Dia."

"No."

"Well. I think we need to get back, get the head, and take it to the medical examiner if he or she is still here."

"I'm not looking forward to that, Stefan."

"Me neither but it has to be done. Look at the side of the building."

She looks to where he is pointing and sees a pile of discarded wooden crates. Most the size of a travel chest. Some with rope handles.

"Let's take one of those, one with the handles. We can put it in there and when we get back, I'll get a hold of Sergeant Booth and he can pick us up. Chuck a few pine boughs in there to cover the stink... or most of it anyway. And then..."

Dia frowns with surprise when he stops talking and rushes to the back row of the parking lot and stops beside a blue and black 1935 Dodge. She follows him. The paint job is terrible. He checks the back fenders. One has a dent.

"Dia, it's the car Carter saw. The killer is on base now."

"He must work here. It makes sense. He would have access to the whole base and the property around it. But the uniform cloth you have. Could it be a serviceman?"

"I don't think Carter's description of a middle-aged man fit the Air Force's requirements and when Booth explained the layout of the base, he told me this is a mainly civilian parking."

Kravchenko returns to the front of the vehicle and places a hand on the hood.

"It's still warm. He must work the late shift."

Kravchenko gets a shivery feeling, the hairs stand on his neck. He turns toward the nearest buildings.

"Someone is watching us."

Dia scans the peripheral of the lot when Kravchenko shouts out.

"There!"

She looks to where he is pointing, and a stocky man stares back at them from the edge of another building with cars and trucks parked in front. He's too far to discern any distinguishing features except for the red and black plaid jacket.

"I see him."

Kravchenko reacts and starts running toward the man. Dia straggles along, still weak from the injury. The man runs. By the time Kravchenko rounds the building and stands in the street, whoever he saw is swallowed up in the activity of the base. Cars coming and going. Heavy trucks and service men everywhere. Planes landing and taking off, the sky abuzz with droning aircraft. Hammers pound heavy metal. Saws echo where workers are adding an addition to one of the storage sheds. The chatter and laughter of men unaware of the dangerous person in their midst. When a truck rumbles away from them, they see the red and black jacket in the dirt and realizing they've lost their quarry. They slow down their pace and stop at the side of the street to wait until another truck goes by before pulling the jacket from the dirt. Kravchenko goes through the two chest pockets and finds nothing.

He's never felt so uneasy. They were so close.

"There are many people on the base. Less on the weekends though, probably cut in half but it never stops. We won't find him now."

Dia is thinking of other things while Kravchenko bemoans the fact that the person they were chasing has evaded them.

"He wasn't in uniform, Stefan. What does that tell us?"

They both come to the same assumption. He voices their thoughts.

"There is more than one person involved. One is a civilian and the other is an airman."

Dia is not familiar enough with the base and unsure of their next move so looks to Kravchenko for direction.

"What are you thinking, Stefan?"

"I need to get a hold of Sergeant Booth."

He turns back toward the repair shop and speaks to the sergeant in charge. The man points to an office in front off to the side, and tells him it is Repair Depot 12. Kravchenko sits at the desk and uses the phone. He has two numbers memorized for Booth and finds him on the first try.

"I'm at the Number Twelve Repair Shed, Sergeant and I need you and an armed serviceman to meet me here on the double."

After a brief pause, he hangs up and makes another call. Issuing another order, he hangs up.

"Let's go outside Dia and wait for Booth. He won't be long."

"What are you planning?"

He leads her to a tanker truck parked to the side of the building. Heavy jacks lift the rear of the vehicle, and two men are wrestling with the set of tandem tires on the opposite side of them. Kravchenko and Dia stand at the hood and can see the parking lot while he talks.

"I'm having a man stand guard, somewhere discrete where he can't be seen, to watch the car. If they work on base, they have to leave at the end of their shift."

She's about to interrupt him when he holds up his hand.

"I know what you're thinking. The man who was running is likely the owner and probably won't return but I'm covering all bases."

"We need to get the evidence in the forest."

"Right. I'll have Booth arrange transfer of the head to the hangar. We need to check the infirmary for any recent injury. I spoke with one of the sentries. The medical examiner was about to leave. We can verify the identity of the other corpse if he's still there."

She folds her arms and leans back on the wide grill of the truck, plunking down on the bumper. She clears her throat, removes her hat and fans her face with it. Kravchenko can see the sweat beading on her forehead although it's not that warm out, starting to cool off gradually with darkness a couple hours away.

"You okay?"

"Yeah, yeah. I had a dizzy spell there for a second. Just need to sit for a minute. We still haven't looked at the photos you're carrying."

Although he's been clinging to them, Kravchenko has forgotten about them. He looks down at the folder with a frown.

"I haven't been thinking of them. We can check them later. We've more important things to do now."

Her hat ends up in her lap and she removes a handkerchief from a back trouser pocket to wipe her brow. Then she puts the hat back on with a smile.

"After I get the plate number, I'll get a call into the station. They'll have to contact the manager of the registration office and get a person on it right away. I need to get a report written up tonight as soon as I can."

"We'll go look at it after I talk to Booth, but I already know who owns the car."

Dia's puzzled look comes with a raised brow.

"You do?"

"Yep. A dead leading aircraftsman from Winnipeg."

44

5:27 pm

After Iron Spear rounded the repair shed, he dumped the jacket, hustled along a passing truck with a load of lumber, fell in with a group of workers and ducked into a building with an open bay door. The front section is a material warehouse and a mill in the back. He walks with a hurried pace toward the mill, greeting a few men he knows. It's not odd for him to be here. He stops looking over his shoulder, manages to lose his pursuer and is finally able to slow down to let his heart settle. The building he works in is next door and can be accessed from the back entries.

He panicked when he saw the airman and a cop by his car. He shouldn't have. What are they looking for? What did they know about the car? If they check the registration, it will throw them off. There's no one working here named Coleman. He can't go back for the car. There is bound to be someone watching it. Maybe he can hitch a ride with Emile the electrician on night duty who lives in Dieppe and goes right by his place. He's not worried, he prepared for this. Nothing will keep him from his mission.

He's sorry he lost the jacket, bought new this afternoon. At least, he's glad he wore a sweater. He hurries his pace. He has a lot to do tonight, and right now he needs to hide the blasting cap and fuse. In his panic, he'd forgotten about it. He calms down and concentrates on his plan. He needs to pick up his tools and the pickup truck and meet Emile, and whoever is his helper tonight, at the work site: the building with the red X.

45

6:01 pm

Kravchenko is finishing up details with Sergeant Booth while Dia searches the vehicle. The Dodge is a big car with a long snout and bug-eye head lights. It's a touring sedan, four doors with suicides in the back. The tires show wear, and the whitewalls are smudged with dark streaks. Opening one of the back doors and swinging it to her right, the first thing she notices is the debris on the floor. The owner has a weakness for potato chips. She guesses there are ten or twelve empty 5 cent bags of Scotties on the floor along with two empty pop bottles and a pair of used and scuffed up leather gloves on the back seat. Dia pokes at them and flips them but doesn't see any blood. The front seat reveals only mud on the floor, another chip bag and a folded *Transcript* in the passenger's seat. She can see yesterday's date. Nothing here. This model doesn't have a dash compartment.

As she closes the door she has to hold herself up on the roofline for a moment. A feeling of fatigue sweeps over her and her head spins, but it doesn't last long. Giving herself a minute, she joins Kravchenko and Sergeant Booth at the entry to the parking lot. She can't help noticing how big Booth is, massive shoulders. She imagines when he barks an order people listen. He's handsome in a rough way, square jaw, the scar by his eye. She wouldn't want to tangle with him. Standing a few steps to the side, she listens to Booth.

"The watchman I posted is on the left corner of the building.

Twelve, thirteen feet toward the tree line there is a stand of young birch."

Booth is a restless type and always moving around. He's pointing to the far corner of the last Hangar No. 9. The forest runs parallel to the side of the building ten feet away. There is no fence, only thick scrub. The airman can't be seen.

"Can he see well enough, Sergeant? You pointed out there are two lights, here at the entry and one behind us at the back."

"Yes sir, I checked it out myself. There is enough visibility to see the whole lot. He knows where the target car is and the entry. Although your description of the individual is vague, Sir.

"Yes, I regret he was too far away to really..."

Dia is struck by a thought and steps closer to the men, waving her palms back and forth.

"Whoa, whoa, guys I remember something odd about when he turned to run away. He had a limp."

Now that she mentions it, Kravchenko remembers the man had an odd gallop, a thicker man, stout, not too tall, darkish short hair, no hat. The jacket caught his eye but that's of no use.

"Add that detail to our watchman, will you Booth? Remember, if the owner returns, the guard is to hold him or subdue him if he needs to. And can you personally look after the other detail I mentioned earlier. As soon as you can. If you need help, take someone who knows how to keep their mouth shut."

"Yes, Sir."

"We're off to get something to eat. We'll meet you later."

"Yes, Sir.

Booth heads in the direction of the airman in the bush. Kravchenko is gabbing away, going over the things they have, mentally putting them in a list.

"Anything in the car, Dia?"

After ten seconds with no answer, he notices Dia lagging behind. By the time he stops and turns to see what's happening, he's too late to catch her from falling.

46

Kravchenko rushes to her side and kneels beside her. Holding her head up, she blinks into the light. She pushes him off, sits up, rubs grit from her hand and wipes the tiny pebbles from her brow where it contacted the ground when she fell. She grabs her hat.

"Whoa. Took a little dizzy spell again. Feels like I scraped my forehead."

Kravchenko helps her stand.

"Yes, there is a scratch over your eye. Maybe we should drop into the infirmary and have someone check your injury."

Brushing the road dust from her rump and trousers, she shakes her head.

"No, no... I'm fine. Let me sit down for a minute."

She sits on the floorboard of a nearby truck and hangs her head, rubbing her temples with one hand, dangling the hat from the other. Kravchenko admires the strong features in her profile. He recalls the moment he impulsively kissed her. He tells himself this is not the right time and place for any romance. He needs to concentrate on the trouble at hand.

"Let's get a quick bite and then we can meet with Sergeant Booth at the hangar. He should've returned with the head by then. "

Booth was on his way out of the back rooms when Kravchenko and Dia meet him inside the hangar past the first guard but before the sawhorse barrier.

"How did it go, Sergeant?"

"It's done, Sir. The head is on ice. Smells terrible and it's not in good shape."

"Thank you, Sergeant. I know it's been a long day, but I need you to do one more thing for me. If no one comes near the car in the parking lot or there's no sign of movement toward it or anything suspicious, have it impounded here in Hangar 5 before daylight."

"Will do. Anything else, Sir?"

"Have you been in contact with GC Clark?"

"No, I have not."

"I need to liaise with him to update our investigation."

"I doubt he's still on base. He usually leaves around six."

"I see. Okay then, carry on, Sergeant."

Booth leaves and they discover the ME has already left as well and will return in the morning. Kravchenko faces Dia, his arms akimbo and a weary look on his face. The guards can see he is thinking hard and they remain silent. He wants to know if Clark alerted the *Baffin*. After a few moments, he realizes there is nothing else they can do tonight. He's overcome with tiredness. He doesn't feel like looking at the head tonight. It's been a long day. After informing the guard of their whereabouts and telling him to radio Booth with the info, he and Dia leave.

"I'll escort you to your car, Inspector Francis."

Once there, she bids him a goodnight and Kravchenko proceeds to the barracks. During the walk, a weird feeling comes over him. Besides being tired, he feels a sense of helplessness and strongly believes something imminent is about to happen.

47

Iron Spear, Emile the electrician and a helper are working on the empty building at the back of the base. The Air Maintenance Squadron Command will be located in the new building slated for occupation at the end of the month. Earlier he planted the fuse and blasting caps he smuggled on to the base in the bottom of the toolbox he leaves on site. When he had arrived and was getting his tools ready, he went to the washroom and removed the items from his thigh.

He and the helper are hanging the interior doors on the new offices. He already knows where he is going to plant the bomb tomorrow night. A gleeful tremor passes through his body each time he thinks of the damage. Once the diversion is created, he will rush to where the direction-finding unit is and force his way inside. He will have two hours to leave the base and rendezvous with the submarine off Cap-de-Cocagne where Elmer Coleman rented the cottage. He has a dory waiting and his escape route planned.

He needs to get a lift home tonight with Emile. He'll tell him his car wouldn't start and that he will have to have it towed in the morning. He's fortunate to have a backup to cover every contingency he could imagine. Elmer Coleman owns more than one car. He only needs to retrieve it from a barn he rents from an old lady. He hopes the car doesn't smell as stale as the dead air he remembers there.

The second thing he needs to deal with is his contact on the base.

The man is starting to panic, complaining he hasn't been paid. Once Iron Spear discovered the man's unsavory secret life, it was easy to blackmail him. What motivated him was money and silence about his depravities. Little does he know he's not going to get what he was promised. Tomorrow night at midnight, Iron Spear will be gone. Today the idiot said he was going to bury the head. Iron Spear told him it didn't matter if they found it. He'll know tonight what happened. They have a rendezvous at one o'clock in the morning. There is only one way to guarantee his silence.

48

Midnight

Oberleutnant Zur See Atzinger has ordered the submarine to remain submerged. He has been surfacing at night to recharge. Moving submerged, they drifted into the strait before dusk and came to periscope depth to check their surroundings and look for threats. They spied a ship leaving the port of Bouctouche, fully laden by the look of her bowline underwater. One of the ships anchored in the bay has moved in to be loaded. There is one more and it is anchored well beyond his planned route of escape. There has been no sign of the sub hunter but he's taking no chances.

He sits in his small cabin finishing his daily log entry. He underlines the sentences reinforcing his decision to postpone the original rendezvous. He knows he will be questioned and reprimanded but the boat is under his command. The safety of his men and the success of the mission are his responsibility. The sub hunter will have moved on. When first sighted it was following the coast north. He knows from his original instructions from the political officer, a mousy creep from Berlin using sources within the Halifax Naval Yard, that there are presently four ships capable of finding and sinking U-boats patrolling the Maritime coastline from northern New Brunswick to Campobello Island in the south and Prince Edward Island. He wants to rationalize where they may be and study once more his route of escape.

From a small shelf wrapped in netting over his bed, he removes a rolled-up collection of papers. He clears off his collapsible desk and unfurls the maps. The one he wants is the second one. Slipping it out of the bunch, he curls up the others and chucks them on his bed. He unrolls the one he has picked out, smooths it out and places a heavy object on each corner. The map displays the eastern coast of New Brunswick from the northeastern tip, which looks like a claw, the island province, and the lobster shape of Nova Scotia. He has marked a route he thinks fastest.

He sailed in around an island called Cape Breton on the tip of Nova Scotia. This time he intends to cut back through St George's Bay, through the Strait of Canso between Cape Breton and the mainland and into the Chedabucto Bay. From there it's open water northeast straight to Europe. His only concern is the gap between the island and the more southerly part of the province. He knows from the maps it's wide enough, but is it deep enough? His experience tells him a body of water with this breadth would have a passable channel, but he intends to sail through at periscope depth in the dark. It is worth the risk, though, as it will save him hours. The moon is waxing and should be two-thirds full. He hopes for a clear night. Yes, it's settled in his mind to go for quicker access to deeper water.

Shortly before midnight tonight he'll surface and rendezvous at the coordinates provided to Iron Spear. Then its onward to the naval base at Bremerhaven in Germany. At best speeds, either submerged or on the surface, the trip is fourteen to fifteen days of straight sailing, twenty-four hours a day. Because the submarine the commands is the newer Type XXIII, his top speed submerged is 11 knots. On the surface, he can move at 13 to 14 knots.

U-boat 498 has a crew of fifty-eight men, including himself. All are loyal to the Reich, all loyal to him. He makes life or death decisions and they look to him with pride and hope. He vows to bring this contact marked ultra-important home as ordered, or to die trying.

49

From the edge of the property of the rented cottage, Iron Spear can see the car approach with no headlights. Few clouds obstruct the nightlight from a pregnant moon. In the northwest the light of the Big Dipper contrasts against the black sky, the tip of its handle pointing to Polaris. The temperature has dropped and there is a chance of frost. He's bundled in a wool knee-length coat. The cottage is in darkness and even though it is isolated, Iron Spear is taking no chances of drawing attention. The dead of night exaggerates the lingering scent of seaweed, salt water and dying foliage.

There is enough light, however, for him to make out the man get out of the car and proceed toward the front door. Iron Spear moves away from the edge of a storage shed to the right of the driveway. Trees overhead hide the starlight and with the moon in the southeast. Only his silhouette is visible, as is the visitor's.

"Over here."

The man's arms flair when he jumps back from the gruff voice calling to him and almost loses his balance.

"Damn! You scared me!"

"Be quiet, and join me."

"Yeah... sure, sure."

The man stumbles through the tall grass for fifty feet, unable to see a path. His nerves are taking a beating as he watches in the shadow for the other man, the one who enjoys killing. His bravado is melting fast, he's scared and he rues the day they met. But $25,000 was too tempting, the danger of exposure too humiliating. He feels a lot more comfortable with the gun in his pocket. Stopping a dozen steps away, his night vision can make out the shape of the body, face hidden by a hat, a fedora with a wide brim. He swallows hard and uses his best commanding voice.

"Did you bring the money?"

The shadow raises an arm with a bladder shaped object hanging from it.

"Yeah, yeah, it's here."

"Just give it to me as you promised. I gave you what you wanted. You have all the information I could get on the magnetron, where it is, how heavily guarded it is, everything you asked for. As much as I hated it, I even helped you with the bodies. When I leave, I never heard of you."

Iron Spear steps closer, two arm lengths away. His bulk overshadows the man who doesn't need to see his face to recognize the aggression.

"Did you go near the head?"

The man won't back down as scared as he is. He pushes himself to exert some authority.

"Yes, yes I did."

"I told you to forget it. It's too risky with people snooping around."

"I thought it would help delay identification. They don't have a lot to go on. You only need another twenty-three hours."

Angrier now, his voice almost a hiss.

"What did you do with it?"

"Nothing. It... it was already discovered."

The man doesn't have a good poker face and is glad for the darkness. He won't say anything about his encounter.

"How do you know?"

"I saw the policewoman and the service man. I was hiding. They couldn't see me."

"You fool. You could've gotten caught. You could've ruined the whole thing. You'd get life in prison. I'd get execution."

The visitor, with slow gestures, slips his hand inside the jacket pocket and takes the grip of the Browning 35 and points it toward the center mass of the German.

"Not my plans either but they have nothing. Now give me my money."

Iron Spear sees the subtle movement and expects a gun. He grips the knife by his side tighter and tosses the canvas sack at the man's feet. He'll wait for him to bend to pick it up. His voice is calmer, almost friendly.

"After tomorrow... I should say tonight, I'll be gone and you can get back to your filthy sex games with your depraved bunch of associates. You should be more careful. If I can find out, I'm sure others can. In Germany you would be in a workcamp."

The gun makes the man bolder.

"Well, we're not in Germany are we. By the way, there is a rumour in the investigation of a submarine. You're the one who should be careful. And I see they found your car. Not smart."

Iron Spear waits him out. Let's his silence speak.

The man steps closer to the bag, a lump in the cluster of grass. With his head up, staring at the German, he bends at the knees, keeping his upper body straight and the gun pointing up. Iron Spear notices the man's head drop to orient the hand reaching down and he strikes out. Misjudging the distance in the dim light, the tip of the blade shears the chest of the man's jacket, opening it like a flesh wound. The man, who was crouching, falls backward from the swipe of the knife and pulls the trigger.

The 9mm bullet hits Iron Spear's forearm a shade above the wrist, where the bones are farthest apart, and cracks the ulna on the way through. The knife flies from his hand and the momentum flips him backward with his head striking the hard ground. Gripping his injured arm to his chest, he grits his teeth in order not to yell out. He can hear running feet but can't give chase. The throbbing arm redirects his thoughts. He needs to get to the cottage. Sitting up he watches the car race out the driveway. He whispers to the night.

"If I had time, I'd kill you slowly."

50

Saturday 7:45 am

Kravchenko and the medical examiner, Dr. Roman Tewksbury, meet in the hangar which everyone concerned is calling the morgue. He has the report Kravchenko wrote up for the GC two days ago. He's written a preliminary report of his own and hands Kravchenko a copy. The ME is a middle-aged man, maybe fifty-five or so with short hair greying along the temples. Laughter lines crease his temples. His eyes are bright and no-nonsense. He doesn't seem to be in a good mood.

"I don't know where you got the pull, Warrant Officer, but this is highly irregular for me to have to come to the bodies. I can only give you summation based on my experience and a visual inspection of the corpses and heads."

"There's a war going on, Doctor. These are extraordinary times and this needs to be an Air Force matter directed out of the Department of Natural Defence for the security of our country. We need you to keep this wrapped tight, the fewer people involved the better until we catch the culprit."

The doctor rues his attitude and it shows on his reddening cheeks.

"Yes, of course."

He turns to page two of his report.

"From what I can glean, the cause of death is obvious, a knife wound to the chest. Taking what I read from your own report and description of the bodies when you found them, the time of death

180

would've been six to seven days ago. The separation of one head was skillfully done, the other more like it was done in a hurry. Cadaver one I estimate to be approximately in the early twenties, the only identifying marks is the oddly shaped ankle and the mole on the back. The other fits into that age group as well with no identifying marks as such. I've matched the heads to the cadavers which I'm sure you also were able to distinguish. The heads are not in good shape and it's hard to distinguish any features other than hair color. I'll know more when the autopsies are done."

Kravchenko interrupts the ME.

"One thing that bothers me is that there were no defensive wounds or what I perceived as such on either body."

"Yes, I noted that as well."

"Makes me think they might've known the killer or that the surprise was total."

"I can only lend a hand with what I see. The rest is up to you detectives."

Kravchenko nods and remembers the detail Lucille Gallant told him about.

"Did you notice anything along the eyebrows of the second head?"

"Yes, now that you mention it. There was a slight area where the hair doesn't grow, probably from an accident in the past. It looks like scar tissue underneath and was likely a cut."

"We were checking on missing persons and it was one thing the sister mentioned. You've confirmed what she told us. So, we now have the identity of the two bodies. I'm not sure the autopsies will tell us anything new."

"It's possible but one never knows. Regardless of the killing wound, a dead body gives up its secrets. I understand the need for secrecy as you've explained to me, and I will have the cadavers and heads transported to the morgue in Moncton. We will follow up with you as soon as we can."

"Excellent."

"I'll make arrangements, and who should I liaise with?"

"Flight Sergeant Wilbur Booth. I'll inform him ASAP and he will be at your disposal. I'll arrange for him to meet you here. Thank you for putting up with these odd circumstances and remember because of the sensitive work being done here, and with the terrible war going on, we need you to keep this information to as few as possible until we tell you different."

"I understand. Happy to be of help."

"Good day doctor. I'll have Sergeant Booth sent right over."

"Good day Warrant Officer Kravchenko."

◻

When he's leaving the hangar, he heads to the mess to meet Dia. When he arrives at the building, he phones instructions to Sergeant Booth. Returning the phone to the receptionist, he's surprised to see Dia coming down the hallway toward him. Small welts dot her forehead, but her smile is uninjured. She waves to Kravchenko.

"Good morning, Stefan. And no falling down jokes, okay?"

He can't help laughing at her seriousness, but her continued glare makes him clear his throat.

"Ahem... good morning to you too, Dia. I would never do that. Are you sure you should be up and about?"

"You're full of baloney. You're not getting rid of me that easy. I'm feeling fine except for a nagging headache. I took a couple of aspirin and I'm ready to get on with our investigation. What's going on?"

Warmth wells up in Kravchenko when he sees she's ok.

"I was going to check up on Carter."

"I did already and he's recovering well. Says he's enjoying all the attention."

Kravchenko is happy with the news and feeling responsible for the young man's plight, he's relieved.

"We can grab something to eat and make our plans for the day."

"Good idea. I'm famished and I need a coffee."

Meat grilling on the fryers and coffee brewing greet them on the way in. After going through the cafeteria, Kravchenko and Dia find a seat near the wall amongst the busy commotion of dozens of people eating before they head off to work. They each have their own tray. His has fried eggs, bacon, toast, and a steaming mug of coffee, hers just toast and a dollop of marmalade and her own mug. During breakfast he explains what the ME said, and that he released the bodies.

"We now have the identity of the two bodies. We need to talk with the families again and associates, look for possible suspects. When I spoke to Booth, he informed me the car has been impounded. There's still no word from GC Clark who I need to speak to as soon as I can. I think we need to split up this morning. If you could contact Lucy Gallant and inform her of her brother, Pierre. Remind her of the secrecy act and tell her where the body is going. Follow up any leads she may give you. I'll talk to the commander and visit the family of Tim Grant."

"All right. How about we meet up here at noon?"

"Perfect. If something comes up to delay either of us, contact Sergeant Booth. Before we take off, I'll inform him of our whereabouts after I speak to the GC."

Dia downs the rest of her coffee and wipes her lips with her napkin. Kravchenko finishes the last of his toast and puts everything back on his tray. Grabbing her tray as well, he stands and hesitates for a moment, and eyes the semi-automatic on her Sam Browne belt.

"Watch your back Dia. Two suspects are roaming the property and things are getting dicey. With the car impounded, the culprit will be using another vehicle or bumming a ride. I wish we had a better description of the man. A limp, that's all we know."

"The other has a torn uniform. That might be something to go on."

"I expect those will have been trashed by now, but who knows."

They dump the trays and leave the building. Kravchenko has the use of an Air Force vehicle parked by the barracks. Dia has hers parked at the infirmary lot. She stops and gets Kravchenko's attention.

"Hey Stefan, did you check the boot prints yet? The photo enlargements? Don't know if they'll tell us anything but still worth looking at."

"Right, I'll do that now before I talk to CG Clark."

They part company outside the mess hall.

Kravchenko returns to Hangar 5 where he left the photos in the conference room. There is an Air Force and a civilian ambulance in the main bay and Tewksbury is arranging for the transfer of the corpses. The car from the parking lot has been impounded. Kravchenko informs the LAC in charge of guard duty that they are no longer needed and can return to regular duty. He orders the man to pass the information onto Sergeant Booth and the rest of the guard detail. Proceeding to the room, he withdraws the photos and studies them closely. The print in the woods matches the boots worn by the first cadaver.

The second print from where the first body was recovered causes him to pause. There's something familiar. Then it strikes him. They are the same as the newer ones he and Dia found just before he left. Whoever removed the first body from the water and the person who made the newest tracks are the same. While trying to decide what this means, he recalls the torn fabric, quite possibly part of an Air Force uniform. Setting the two photos on the table, he lifts his own heel behind the other leg and grabs it so he can see it better. It's a flat heel, plain in the center but around the edge is raised ridge, shaped like a horseshoe. Same as in the photo.

The only difference between his heel and the one in the photo is that his are newer. He drops his foot, and propping himself up with both hands on the edge of the table, he bends to stare closer at the photos. In one the ridge of the heel is worn badly at the back on the outside. In another he discovers the same on the opposite one, which he believes is the right foot. Could it mean the person is bowlegged? he questions. Tuck that thought away. Kravchenko can't recall any clearer details but recalls that the ridge from the fresh ones yesterday was unbroken. He'll tell Dia about it later and get her thoughts. They might have to go back and do a quick check. He puts the photos back into the crumpled brown envelope.

"Must be a couple hundred pairs of boots with those heels. Don't know if it'll help but it's one more thing we know about the killer."

Tucking the envelope under his arm, he straightens his uniform jacket and puts his hat back on, tipped forward over the right brow, and leaves for Group Captain Clark's office. He hopes the commander has alerted the *Baffin*. His initial feelings from dealing with Clark is the man is new in the command with a big ego and is worried about how he's going to come out of this. No doubt he'll take the credit for any success. When Kravchenko arrives at the main office, he's determined not to worry about the man's ego or his future ambitions. He'll override him with a higher authority if he has to and it won't take much begging with two headless bodies.

51

Kravchenko removes his hat and slides it into the left epaulet of his uniform jacket as per regulations and enters the office to find the Group Captain sitting in one of the leather chairs off to the right of his desk like last time. A couch rests under a boasting wall lined with his photos and diplomas. Another chair is at the end of the couch facing the GC. He greets Kravchenko with a smile. It's a rare sight and looks forced. Right away Kravchenko wonders what he's up to. Clark waves his hand at the second chair.

"Have a seat, Warrant Officer."

"Thank you, Sir."

There is a pot of coffee and mugs on a side table. Clark points to them.

"Would you care for a coffee before you bring me up to date?"

"No thank you, Sir. I've already had several."

"Fine. Now what's happening with your investigation, Kravchenko?"

Kravchenko settles himself in the chair and removes a notebook from an inside pocket of his uniform jacket.

"Before I start sir, did you contact *HMCS Baffin*?"

"All looked after. I received word from the captain that there have been no sightings on their patrol, and that he will keep me advised."

Kravchenko is bewildered by the look on the commander's face. In his brief experience, Clark is not normally so compliant and never with a smiling face.

"Shall I contact the captain myself, Sir? To let him know what we saw?"

The smile disappears and the sour look returns. Kravchenko's more comfortable with this side of Clark.

"Not necessary, Warrant Officer. I've relayed the information exactly as you explained to me. I was adamant in my request to be vigilant. I'm sure this is their field of expertise and I trust the captain's judgement, as you should trust mine."

"Yes, Sir."

"Carry on."

Kravchenko goes through his notes briefly and reads off the points he wanted to discuss.

"The bad news is we..., me and Inspector Francis of the RCMP... believe the killer is an employee here on the base. Yesterday Inspector Francis was assailed by an unknown opponent we believe is working with the perpetrator which would explain his familiarity with the base. It is someone in uniform."

Kravchenko looks up at Clark to gauge his reaction and is surprised to see there is none. His face remains stoic. He does inquire about Dia.

"Is the Inspector all right?"

"She's fine except for a headache. I tried to convince her to take a break and rest up but that is not the Inspector's way. She is already off base to question family members of one of the bodies we have identified."

"So, you have been able to identify them. Excellent Kravchenko. And who are they?"

"Both local people. Tim Grant is the first body and the second is a young man named Pierre Gallant. Both men probably caught the culprit unaware and he retaliated by killing them."

He goes on to explain the findings from the ME. He tells him about Carter and the auto.

"... and we recovered the car we believe the killer used."

"Were you able to trace anything from the auto?"

"We haven't gone through it as completely as we'd like but there was nothing of help at our first look. Dia has someone working on the registration, but I already know where that will lead us."

"And where will that lead us?"

Kravchenko relays the information he's garnered about Elmer Coleman. After he completes his report, he offers his opinion that they should be prepared for something major to happen in the next twenty-four to forty-eight hours. Clark sits quietly rubbing his chin and thinking. Kravchenko remains silent.

"How can you be so specific?"

"It's a gut feeling, Sir. Especially since we've discovered the vehicle. The magnetron has to be the reason for the subterfuge."

"What are your next steps?"

"I will be following up on the identity of the first body by questioning family and associates, looking for leads to who the base employee might be, who they know that works here, anything to track him down. We're planning on working with the personnel department on any employees with the vague description I have. I am having Sergeant Booth look for any suspicious activity or questionable actions by any member of the Air Force here on base."

"Why?"

"We believe the second person involved is a member of the Air Force."

"How so?"

Kravchenko tells Clark about the material on the broken branch, the piece of skin, the blood and how painful the injury must be.

"He'll be favoring that leg for sure."

"This bothers me greatly, Kravchenko. One of our own members in cahoots with a killer and him an employee. We need to wrap this up and catch the bastards. I am in touch with my commanding officer, and I can tell you he is not happy. The magnetron must be protected at all costs. There are only a few more tests to be done and the results to be relayed to our counterparts in England. Do you understand?"

"Yes, Sir."

"Now, would you be so kind to fetch me another cup of coffee?"

Kravchenko beetles his brows. It's an odd request. Clark sees his questioning look.

"I had an appointment off base yesterday afternoon, and I fell, twisting my knee, and that is why you find me here in this chair. My whole leg is very uncomfortable, and the doctor told me to use it as little as possible."

Kravchenko pours another mug of steaming java and looks askance at the GC.

"Cream and sugar?"

"Just a dab of cream if you will. Thank you."

Kravchenko passes the cup to his superior officer and can't help noticing the drops of blood by the commander's right foot. The GC seems unaware of it.

"Did you cut your leg, Sir?"

"Oh no. Just gave it a twist. Carry on Kravchenko."

"Yes, Sir."

The blood droplets are foremost in his mind as he leaves the office. Why is the GC lying? He's probably embarrassed at his incapacity and trying to play down his injury. He knows the type. Can't be seen as weak with his underlings. Kravchenko realizes he has no time to ponder on it. He needs to get going. Time to question the Grants and others, and then meet Dia at noon.

52

Iron Spear fled from the cottage after gobbing antiseptic on his injury. He bundled his lower arm in a towel and returned to Scoudouc where he had a better first-aid kit. This morning his arm throbs and the hand is swollen. He's treated the wounds with peroxide and the sting was almost unbearable. He wraps the wounded arm as snug and secure as possible. Thanks to the methadone pills, he can handle the discomfort, though he's careful taking them having been warned they're addictive. He's been nursing his arm all morning and it should be rested long enough. It is time to go get his vehicle.

Taking one of his socks, he cuts the foot off and pulls the leg part over the bandage taking care not to undo it. A dull ache accompanies the action. The sock fits from the middle of the forearm to the middle of the upper arm and holds the bandage in place. He hugs it close to his chest with a makeshift sling. His jacket covers his arm and the sleeve of his coat hangs loosely by the side.

The barn where his other vehicle is stored is owned by Martha Dobbins of Malakoff, a village three miles from his house. He has to walk to pick up the car. The Dobbins' house and barn are set back from the road which bends south to Memramcook. The nearest neighbour is a quarter mile away. Paid for six months in advance, it has been perfect for his needs. He hates to disturb the old lady, but she has the key to the padlock and she doesn't trust it to anyone.

After knocking on her front door and waiting several minutes, he's greeted by a short woman, in slippers, wearing a dark skirt and a beige turtleneck sweater with a black knitted shawl covering her shoulders. She accompanies him to the barn and asks him to help her swing the large door open wide enough to get his '37 Plymouth out. Looking around inside, he notices two more vehicles, one of them going nowhere. It sits up on blocks, the hood missing. Like his, it's covered with a thick blanket of dust. The woman is rambling on about the war in a voice as tiny as she is.

"We're starting to hear awful things about how the Jews are being treated in Europe. A terrible situation, don't you think, Mr. Coleman?"

"I expect they are only rumours, Mrs. Dobbins. Not to worry. We're safe here. Is your son home today?"

"No, he had to take a load of pulp for one of our neighbours to the stock yards in Richibucto. Should be back later this afternoon. Will you be returning the car, or can I rent the space out to someone else?"

"No, I'll be using this car over the winter. Sold my other car yesterday."

She looks at him with beady eyes and a wrinkled face.

"There's no refund on your deposit."

He smiles and shakes his head.

"I understand. You made that quite clear when I first talked to you. There is only two months left so please keep it as my way of saying thank you."

A satisfied smirk crosses her narrow face, and she stands aside as he wipes the dust from the windshield, the shawl held closed with one hand and the other clutching the padlock. She notices he is only using his left arm, the other a harmless sleeves swinging.

"Did you hurt your arm, Mr. Coleman?"

Iron Spear experiences a pang of panic. The question is a grim reminder of the incident in the night. Anger rises from somewhere deep inside of him at the escaping airman and the old lady's nosiness. He pays attention to the auto and counts backwards from twenty to cool his temper. *Zwanzig, neunzehn, achtzehn...*

He's always been like that, easily provoked, often by simple gestures or comments. It's his one weakness and he works to control his killing urges. He looks at her with eyes of frost and she notices it.

"Yes, I fell yesterday evening and twisted my elbow. It's feeling stiff and it hurts when I use it so I have it in a sling, mostly for comfort."

He forces a smile when he sees her uneasiness.

"It was painful during the night and I didn't sleep well. I'm mad at myself for being so clumsy."

She relaxes a little but decides then she doesn't like this man and, uncomfortable in his presence, moves outside by the door.

Iron Spear ignores her and gets in. The key is still in the ignition where she insisted it stay in the event her son had to move the car. When he tries it, he discovers the battery is dead.

"*Scheiße!*"

It was loud enough for her to hear. Her mother was of German descent and Dobbins heard the word often while growing up. It was her mother's much used and only curse word. She frowns at her confusion and feels a moment of fear for a reason she can't understand.

"Do you speak German, Mr. Coleman?"

He gets out of the car and looks at her with a fierce glare. The man's demeanor makes her nervous. The dead battery and the woman's question cause his anger to flare, and he rushes her. Taken aback at his aggressiveness, she drops the shawl and turns to run back to the house, but her short legs are no match for his aggression. He grabs her from behind with his good arm, catching her by the head, his hand covering her mouth. Pulling her close to his side, he drags her back into the barn. Her screams are muffled. She beats at his hand with her tiny fists but he's too strong. Throwing her backward on the hay littered planks, he crushes her chest with one knee and grabs her by the neck with his large fingers. Her weak scream echoes in the barn and flows out the door unheard. There is no one within miles to come to her rescue. Her eyes bug out as she pummels his face, his chest, and his sore arm. The pain intensifies from his vise-like grip which soon cuts off her air supply completely. He smiles as he looks directly in her eyes and can feel her fear. It takes thirty seconds for her to die.

Standing back from the body, he closes his eyes and breaths deeply, the rush he gets from killing pulsating through his body, adrenaline soothing his aching arms. Looking down at her, he speaks to the lifeless body.

"You should've minded your own business."

Waiting for his heart to slow down, he worries about the dead battery and wonders what he's going to do. As he checks the walls, he spies a set of crude shelves holding motor parts and tools. On the bottom shelf is a coiled fiber-covered cord with alligator grips on each end, one with a red dot on the handle and the other black. He remembers that on the walk from the house when he arrived there was a red tractor parked at the far side of the barn. He hustles over and with a flush of relief finds the key in the ignition. He thinks these trusting country people stupid.

With the Plymouth running and parked idling by the house, Iron Spear returns to the barn. He drags the old woman's body behind the immobile car and dumps her amid a pile of tires. The movement disturbs the chafe and motes swirl like acrobats and fill the air. He picks up the padlock on his way out. Pocketing the key, he shoulders the tall door shut, loops the hasps together and secures it with the lock. Before he gets back in the car, he takes two more methadone tablets. Removing his sling and sliding the arm back in his jacket hurts. He sets his jaw and bites down until he can hold his hand free. The fingers still move but not without major discomfort. He drops his hand in his lap and waits for the drugs to have an effect. It doesn't take long.

Backing the car out onto the dirt road, he marvels at how little traffic comes this way. Perfect. He'll get to the next task on his list. Iron Spear knows where the *dummkopf* he now has to deal with lives. The man could endanger his mission. Plus his disappearance will improve his plans for tonight, create greater chaos. He's got enough time. Maybe the idiot is home. He doubts it but is going to check.

53

Dia sits at a corner table in the mess hall waiting for Kravchenko and is about to check her watch when she spies him entering the premises, looking around for her in the tumult of hungry people. Some of them are rudely staring at her dark rimmed eyes. Without needing a mirror, she guesses she looks a mess. She has her note pad opened on the table, a half empty mug, a dinner plate smeared with tomato sauce and a few elbows of pasta, and a smaller plate with a piece of apple pie. She waves to Kravchenko, and he holds up a finger and points to the lineup in the cafeteria section. She nods and starts in on her pie.

"How did your morning go, Dia?"

"Well, other than having to tell Lucille about her brother, it went well enough. I spoke to the mother. The father is deceased. It was quite emotional, as you can imagine, but Lucille was able to leave work and go with me to her mother's house. I then spoke to the neighbours. Nothing suspicious. No enemies. Good person. Same stories. They do know people who work on the base, but it is family or neighbours and all vouched for. Excuse me while I finish my pie."

Kravchenko, chewing on his liver and onions, pokes at the mashed potatoes. There's a buzz of conversation, chairs sliding in and out of the tables, cooks shouting orders, so he listens with his head held closer. He's watching her and then she looks up with a mouthful of pie, lips formed into a tight smile and her eyes closed. The dessert must be good. When she looks at him her eyes have a mischievous spark, an *up-to-something* expression.

"There's more, isn't there?"

Nodding, she takes a sip of her cold coffee.

"Yes. Lucy told me to chat with Pierre's best friend, which I did the last interview before I came here. I found him at work. He's camped out with Pierre before but doesn't care for it. They did indeed use the campsite where we found his belongings."

Kravchenko gives her his full attention, his meal forgotten.

"I asked him if Pierre or himself saw anything strange when they used the trail or the campsite. The only thing he could recall was Pierre took off for a few days in the spring. He saw a uniformed man carry what looked like a suitcase going into the woods. Pierre was walking the edge of the field along the tree line and was unseen. The man left carrying a shovel."

She pauses, giving him a minute to digest it. He sees where she's going.

"Whoever buried the object was from the base."

"And get this. He had to have had access to the gates of the property entrance to access the government property. The person had some authority. And there was a car there."

"Did he give you a description of the man or the car?"

"No, he couldn't remember much of what Pierre told him, only that the man was not too tall and in a uniform."

Kravchenko sets down his knife and fork and slides his plate away. He places both elbows on the table and worries his chin with one hand. His knitted brow tells her to wait out his thoughts. While she goes over her notes again, she watches him out of the corner of her eye. She likes the sharp outline of his rugged face and his healthy tan. He's staring at some point in the middle of the table. It's not long until he looks up at her with a puzzled expression, and he speaks low enough so as not to be heard by those at the next tables.

"This might sound odd, Dia, but as soon as you said the words not too tall, my immediate thought was of the GC. And then I recalled being in his office this morning. He said he twisted his knee yesterday afternoon when he was out for an appointment. He spoke to me from one of the casual chairs in front of his desk. Before I left he asked me to get him a cup of coffee as he was nursing his right leg. When I did so, I noticed blood drops on the carpet by his foot. I asked him if he cut his leg and he denied it. I didn't think anything of it until now."

Dia is sitting up straight, leaning ahead, thoughts connecting.

"You think he might've been the one who struck me in the woods?"

"The blood drops. Right leg. We found the cloth on a tree on the right side of the trail. It's a good chance whoever it was had to have been injured on the right side. It could be but it seems a stretch. What could be his motive? Was he involved in the bodies? He's given me free rein. Is he not afraid I would discover his connection?"

Dia is nodding at every sentence.

"It fits when you put everything together. Not too tall. Authority for the gate. Knows about the magnetron. Wanting the investigation kept on the base. Maybe he plans on stealing it… or selling it."

The look each other in the eyes.

"You thinking what I'm thinking, Stefan?"

"Yep. Money."

Kravchenko is shaking his head.

"It can't be. I can't believe he would've risen so high in the ranks and betray his country, be a traitor. Now when there's a war on."

Dia raises her hands in a questioning gesture.

"Who knows what drives a person? We have to follow this up, Stefan. It's a good possibility."

"You're right. I can't just waltz in there though and question my superior officer, especially without proof."

She sits up and sticks out her chin.

"I can."

He beams a broad smile at her gusto and her defensive manner.

"I don't think that's a good idea at this point. What would you ask him? Using the muscle he has as the commander of this base and the deep secret, he can probably override you and have you removed from the base. No, Dia, we need proof."

She sits back in a pout from disappointment.

"Where would we get proof? We can't look around his office."

"His house, maybe. He's a bachelor, divorced I think Booth told me. A house is provided near here for the commander. Government property. He moved there when he transferred in."

"How would we get inside? It's bound to be locked. I can't get a warrant right away and I doubt what we have..."

She stops when she sees the smirk on his face. She can read him so easily.

"I'm not breaking in there. I'm a police officer. I can't go around forcing my way into people's homes."

He straightens his back and sticks his own chin out like she did previously.

"I can."

She laughs at his gesture and waves him off.

"I've been given carte blanche on my investigation, Dia."

He stands, winking at her.

"I'm worried the killer may be targeting the commander. We'd better check his place out for anything suspicious."

"Where is this house, Stefan?"

"I don't know exactly but I'll find out. Let's go."

54

Group Captain Clark's house sits farther afield than others along the main cluster of homes lining the road to Moncton. Scoudouc's core centers around the school and church. A repair garage with gas pumps, a general store and the post office share the village activity. A half a mile from the church going north, train tracks split the road diagonally from a spur line into the base. Homes spread out in each direction, thinning into farms and wide-open spaces.

Booth gave them directions and they watch for a hedge of evergreens about waist high on a well-kept lawn. A neighbour's house sits closer to the road, white shingles, and green trim. Booth said they couldn't miss it. A shaded driveway follows the hedge and goes past the white house up a slight rise to Clark's place.

The green trim sticks out like a beacon, and she slows her auto to enter the private road, basically two worn paths with grass between and on the shoulders. Tall fir trees line the side, spaced evenly apart, for the hundred feet in. Grey clouds have moved on and an autumn sun makes dapples of light on their car. Dia motors along at a slow pace, both she and Kravchenko watching for any sign the GC might be here even though his auto is at the base. When they clear the trees, a bungalow style home appears with a front porch from end to end on the long side. Another hedge separates the property. The back and right sides are wooded, mostly hardwoods, half naked of their colored robes. The left side opens to a field with several houses along the road.

There is nothing on the porch. Nothing in the yard. Curtains in all the rooms are drawn tight. The lawn has recently been cut and fall foliage raked up. Maintenance from the base would look after that. The predominant colours are beige and brown. The open porch is weathered wood. Its two steps meet a stone walkway. Tire tracks decorate a gravel area to the left. A walkway of similar stonework leads to the back of the house. Dia stops the car at the edge of the porch.

They get out studying the terrain, taking note of the way they came in and the front and side of the house. Dia meets Kravchenko on his side.

"What do you think, Stefan?"

"Maybe he left the door open."

"Sure. He knew we were coming, joker."

Her jest gets a chuckle, and he waves her to follow.

They check the front door, a wooden slab that appears it might survive a grenade. Locked. They walk the length of the porch in both directions. To the right is a small window high up, likely a bathroom Kravchenko guesses. The last one is larger, shrouded inside. Dia suggests a bedroom. In the opposite direction after the door there is a large picture window. The curtains are drawn but the edge of one of them is folded over and allows a glimpse into the room. Kravchenko bends to look in but the room is mostly in darkness.

"Can't see anything in there."

"Wonder why he has the curtains drawn. It's as if he is hiding something."

Kravchenko is thinking the same thing.

"Let's check out back."

He points to the opposite side of the house.

"You go that way and I'll meet you in the rear."

They check each side, treading carefully so as not to disturb anything, and meet in the center of the house where a small stoop sits and offers a back door. It is a thick slab, same as the front. Locked. A medium sized window with no curtains is situated between the door and the driveway. It's wider than it is high. Dia stands with her hands on her hips at the foot of the two steps to the ground.

"Nothing to see here either. Wish we could get inside."

Kravchenko doesn't reply. Behind them, a narrow lawn separates the back from a wooded area. The trees are mostly hardwoods with the exception of a cluster of fir trees in the center. The largest one has a rough tree house ten feet off the ground supported by three large limbs. The boards used on the sides are as grey as the decking out front, the colour of an old man's beard. A ladder leans against the tree below an opening into the tree house. Kravchenko trots over and brings it under the window. The ground is uneven and the ladder rocks back and forth.

"Come hold this, Dia, and I'll have a look."

She comes to his side and grips the rough poles of the uprights while he climbs the four rungs to look in the bottom pane.

"It's the kitchen as I expected. Looks like he's a tidy person."

"Is it locked?"

"Yep. Real tight."

He looks down at her and raises his brow in a questioning manner. Thinking of her career if this goes wrong, she gives a reluctant nod. Participating on a break and enter will not look good on her file.

"Okay. I've got the ladder balanced. Step back."

Shielding his face, he uses his elbow to break the glass. Splintered shards tinkle into the sink and onto the ground. He removes a pointed remnant from the bottom of the sash and reaches in to unlatch the window. Sliding it up, he steps up higher on the ladder so he can swing his leg in and get inside. Jumping off the countertop, he walks over to the door and unlocks it. Dia enters and follows Kravchenko, leaving the door open. The kitchen is small and opens to a dining room which has an archway to the living room and the front of the house. Dia comments on the how neat it is.

"Hardly looks lived in, it's so clean. Compulsive behaviour, you think?"

"Could be. His office is the same. Let's look around."

They check the rooms with great attention, first the bathroom and the two bedrooms, finding no evidence of anything foul. There is a door in the hallway which leads to a basement. Proceeding downstairs, they find an unfinished area. On the left is a furnace, water pump and electrical panel, all the utilities in one spot. Close by is a crude bench with paint cans, brushes, a roller with an empty spool. A few hand tools are next to them lined up in order. Several boxes are piled by the opposite wall. On the same side, midway toward the back is a washing machine, a newer model with a square body, stout legs, and a fancy wringer. It sits in front of a sink with taps. A wicker basket of laundry awaits unloading. Next to it is a covered garbage can.

Towards the back is an unfinished wall of gyprock and two doors. Only one has a lock. Glancing at all the objects, they check the boxes, the basket of laundry and then the garbage can. Dia is digging through the contents when she pulls out a pair of Air Force trousers.

"Oh, oh! Look, Stefan."

She holds the right leg of the trousers up where a section is torn off.

"It's the proof we need."

"This is good, Dia. But I'm not sure a torn leg is enough. Set them aside and let's keep looking."

It's then he spies several pairs of shoes and boots in another box. The top pair are uniform boots just like his. He inspects the heel as he lifts them out. The outer ridge is the exact opposite of the image he remembers from the photo. They're the same.

"The boot heel matches the prints around the hole in the ground."

Dia experiences a flushed feeling and her skin tingles.

"It was him. Do you think he's the killer?"

"No, I don't. More of an accomplice I bet. We still have the Dodge and Carter's injury and we know they weren't Clark. The man running from the parking lot yesterday was not Clark either. He's probably giving the killer inside information. Why would he do it, though? I don't understand."

"It has to be money or blackmail."

They both eye the door to the room at the back. After choosing the one on the right, they find that it's pitch dark when Dia opens it. Finding a switch, a red light fills the tiny room. Kravchenko has seen these layouts before.

"A darkroom. The GC is a photographer too. Interesting. Let's try the other room."

Kravchenko lifts the heavy lock in his hand.

Check out this lock, Dia. It's solid looking."

"Yeah, but we need to get inside there. I think we have enough evidence in hand to go one step further. Are you in?"

"No turning back now."

Kravchenko searches for something to leverage against the lock which is held to the door jamb through a hasp. Rushing to the bench, he moves the tools around, finds a hammer and returns to the mysterious door. Using the claws on the hammer, he drives it under the hasp and pries. Four screws hold it, and it barely moves at first. He raises the hammer, drives the claws in deeper and heaves on the handle. The screws pull up splinters as they emerge from solid wood. The hasp pops off and the lock hangs down, useless. Kravchenko drops the hammer and opens the door. Dia moves closer behind him. No light escapes and all they can see is the concrete floor. Reaching inside, Kravchenko finds a switch and flips it on.

Kravchenko's jaw drops and Dia gasps aloud. Both of them have the same thought and say it together. "Blackmail."

55

Iron Spear steers his car into Clark's driveway and when he is almost clear of the trees, he spies another auto near the house and stops. It's not Clark's. Slapping his hand on the steering wheel, he curses his luck. He desperately hoped the man would be here alone so he could finish it once and for all. He decides to park his auto further down the street and come up to the house from the vacant field. There is a tree line from the main road separating the property and he can sneak along there to watch the house. If Clark happens to be alone inside, he can hustle over and finish him.

He's about to turn around so he can see to back up his car when Kravchenko and Dia emerge from the back of the house with items in their arms. They are things he can't identify but the man looks like he's carrying a pair of boots. From their uniforms and stature, he recognizes them from the parking lot last night. More cursing. He needs to get away quickly before they see him but he's too late. He catches them glancing at his car. Backing up as fast as he can, he skids onto the street, almost hitting another vehicle which swerves and speeds around him with the horn blaring.

Kravchenko is holding the torn trousers and the boots from the garbage can. Dia has a cardboard carton, the size of a bread box in her hands. They notice the dark car at the edge of the trees in the driveway at the same time. Not close enough to discern who it is but the wide head is enough for Kravchenko to think of the man running from the parking lot.

"I think it's the man we saw last night leaving the Dodge. Get in quick, Dia, and we'll go after him."

She opens the back door, sets the box on the seat and tosses him the keys.

"You drive."

He flips the trousers and boots into the back and spins the car around on the lawn. By the time they reach the road, the other car is only a dot going toward Moncton. Kravchenko doesn't even slow down as he swerves onto the road and the car slues and straightens out. Dia is holding onto the dash and the armrest.

"I don't think you can catch him, Stefan, he has too much of a gain on us."

"Maybe, but I'm going to try. Hold tight."

The road twists and turns into a wooded section. They catch a glimpse of the auto when they are on a straight stretch but they're not getting any closer. The vehicle disappears around a long bend to the right, a quarter mile away. By the time Kravchenko steers into the turn, they are directly behind a wagon loaded with logs being pulled by a team of four horses. He has to brake hard due to an oncoming truck and the car veers and catches the edge of the road almost going into the ditch. The abrupt sideways action causes one of the back tires to burst and it goes flat. The car rocks from the sudden stop and it's Kravchenko's turn to hammer the steering wheel with his fist.

"Damn! We'll never catch him now."

Dia's heart is racing. She was watching the deep ditch when the car swerved toward the pitch. In a flash she pictured their auto rolling down the incline. She sits back with her hands on her chest.

"That was too close, Stefan. I don't know how you kept it on the road."

"Luck. That's all it was."

They're disturbed by the driver of the truck, a man with a shaggy beard who saw what happened in his rearview mirror. He taps on the window and Kravchenko gets out.

"You okay, Mister?"

"Yeah, yeah, we're fine. Going too fast, I guess. Didn't expect to see a wagon when we came around the bend."

"Anything I can help with? I see your back tire is flat. Got a spare?"

Kravchenko looks to Dia who has joined him on the driver's side. She shrugs her shoulders.

"I don't know. Let's check the trunk."

They open it up and a spare is nestled in the center under a faux floor, the car jack affixed to the center of the rim. Kravchenko turns to the man.

"We're fine. Thanks for stopping."

The driver doffs his hat and smiles at the pretty lady, returns to his truck and heads toward Scoudouc. Because it's warmer now, Kravchenko chucks his uniform jacket in the driver's seat and changes the tire. Dia chatters while he works and listens.

"Did you notice the make of the car?"

"A Plymouth, I think. Or a Dodge. Not new. Looked dark brown but with the light on it might've been burgundy. Not sure."

"If that was the man we think might be responsible for the two dead bodies, what do you think he was doing at Carter's place?"

"Can't answer that but it goes a long way to proving our theory about the GC. He's involved somehow. As soon as I get this changed, we're going to confront him. If the trousers aren't enough, what you have in the box will make him talk."

56

3:36 pm

Iron Spear only slows down when he's certain no one is in pursuit. He enters the town of Dieppe which borders Moncton and drives east back to Scoudouc. He has to return to his house and get ready for work. His last night. The dynamite is carefully concealed in the false thermos.

He curses at himself for coming too close to getting caught. He can't fail his mission. He decides killing Clark will have to wait or be forgotten. He needs to concentrate fully on his objective to obtain his knife, gun, fuses and blasting caps, plant the dynamite, set the fuse, and get into position to take advantage of the confusion. Everything has been rehearsed and planned as best as possible. But like all plans, the unexpected can ruin everything. Only he and Emile are working in the building tonight. He may have to eliminate the electrician.

As soon as he gets to the base, he'll have to explain the new car. When he sneaked a look the Dodge was gone the next day. No one mentioned anything. He'll stash his car in the carpenter's shop. He got permission from the day supervisor when he asked if he could have some of the scrap lumber pieces being thrown out to use as kindling this winter. Then he will take the truck and tools and dynamite to where he is working. At exactly nine-fifty tonight, he will plant the dynamite. At ten he will light the fuse and will have enough time to be where he plans on being when the explosion happens.

During the confusion he will steal the magnetron and hightail it

206

back to the carpenter's shop and leave. There shouldn't be any problem at the gate as the civilians will be evacuated and the base locked up tight. He'll head for Cap-de-Cocagne and row into the strait to wait for the submarine. He can't wait to return to the glorious fatherland.

The only thing he worries about is the nosy cop and her friend. With a shiver of delight, he wonders if he'll have to kill them too.

57

Dia has driven back after the tire was changed. They are sitting in the car outside the main office building on the base. She turns off the ignition and sits back.

"How do you want to handle this, Stefan?"

"I don't think we should give him any warning. Just bypass his aide in the outer office and surprise him with our presence. Bring the box and I'll bring the rest."

They enter the building, bypassing the receptionist and proceed along a lengthy hallway until they reach the end where the GC's offices are located. Entering the outer office, LAC Bancroft, the aide, looks up from his desk and is about to greet the duo when they rush past him much to his protestations, and enter the GC's office to find him at his desk. With a startled look, Clark frowns at the pair. He waves his aide off.

"What's the meaning of you two bursting in here?"

Kravchenko chucks the trousers and boots on the GC's desk, knocking papers askew and on to the floor. Clark forces his wheeled chair back and goes pale.

"You're the one who struck the inspector. You're the one who has been helping the person doing the killing."

Clark stands, the bad leg forgotten.

"How dare you! What you're suggesting is ludicrous. You will pay for your insubordination, Kravchenko."

"I don't think so. We found these in your house. The boot prints match those at the site where something was dug up, where the killing took place."

Clark has an incredulous look on his face, anger rising from deep inside.

"What were you doing in my house? You are in a lot of trouble for entering my premises without a warrant."

Kravchenko points to Dia.

"She might've been, but it was me who broke in. I did so with the authority vested in me and with your approval telling me to do whatever was needed to solve this case. She will be doing the arresting."

Clark scoffs at the remark, taking a relaxed approach even though his forehead is beginning to bead, his leg ache.

"Those are just trousers and boots you have planted at my house. You can't possibly think I killed those two people. Why would you even consider such folly?"

Dia walks over to the GC's desk and dumps the contents from the box on it. Dozens of black and white photos, all enlargements, of Clark wearing ladies under clothing and lingerie, of he and other men in various stages of undress and sexual liaison, closeups of male anatomy. Clark stares at them open-mouthed, his Adam's apple bobbing, rubbing his sweaty palms on his trousers.

"I...I..."

He sags in his chair, chin on his chest, resignation and ruin written on a long face.

Kravchenko looks at him in disgust, not for his deviancies but for his traitorous act - to him, to everyone, to his country. Tight-lipped, he nods to Dia.

Dia removes a pair of handcuffs. Clark sits up.

"Please, leave me some dignity. I'm a commanding officer. Not in cuffs. I'll go peacefully. I'll tell you everything but no handcuffs. Please."

Dia looks to her partner. Kravchenko stands over Clark, his fists curled. Clark shrinks into the chair, his knees trembling.

"Whoever you're helping has come for the magnetron. Tell us who and when?"

"He's... he's a civilian employee, one of the maintenance people. Tonight. That's all I know."

Kravchenko knows he's lying. He would like to beat it out of him. He has to calm down. Dia sees it's time for her to exert her authority.

"Stefan, stand down. This man has broken the law. I'm arresting him. Stand aside while I inform him of his rights."

Kravchenko backs off, never taking his eyes off the GC. Clark sits up straighter with unwarranted bravado.

"With no cuffs, please."

"I'm still thinking about it."

She rattles off by rote what the Group Captain can and cannot do, his right to remain silent, entitled to a lawyer, *et al*.

"Stand up and get your jacket and hat. Do you have a weapon?"

Standing, putting his weight on his good leg, he shakes his head.

"Not on me. One in my desk, bottom drawer, my service revolver."

Kravchenko waves him away from the desk and confirms the gun. Finding the chamber and magazine empty, he lays it on the desk. Clark is two steps from Dia near the front of the desk and points to a narrow door on the wall behind the desk.

"I must appeal to your good nature. I need to use my washroom. I beg of you. I would not want to befoul myself in front of my men."

Dia doesn't feel sorry for the man and won't be put off by his hang dog demeanor. He doesn't deserve any special treatment but it would not be good if the man shits his pants. She goes to check what is behind the door and finds a sink and toilet bowl tucked in a well-appointed space. She checks the room, scans inside the vanity, on the shelf of hand towels, behind the bowl and finding nothing, nods him in. Kravchenko waits in the middle of the room and says, "leave the door open."

The GC offers a weak nod and shuffles to the washroom. Dia follows him and leans her back against the wall beside the door. She can hear him. The unzipping of his trousers, the rustle of clothing being moved and the plunk onto the seat. A lengthy fart causes her to titter and Kravchenko holds his nose and waves the air in jest. She holds her hand over her mouth to stop herself from laughing when she hers something clatter in the washroom. Straightening up, she is about to check when a gun blast pierces the air, startling both of them. She rushes in to find the GC's body slumped over the bowl, his head hanging between his knees, blood dripping on his boots.

The vanity door is open. A bottle of mouthwash rests on its side on the floor in front. A smoking Enfield revolver is still clutched in the GC's hand. The back of his head is missing. Dia is revolted by the sight and Kravchenko shakes his head. They are both interrupted by the door bursting open with LAC Bancroft rushing into the room. Kravchenko pulls the bathroom door shut.

"What's going on? What was that gunshot?"

The commotion brings others to the office. Kravchenko urges LAC Bancroft to get things back under control and issues orders to the man.

"Get everyone back to their work. The GC's injured. Accidental discharge. Cordon this office and don't let anyone in here except us. Tell everyone this is a military matter. Get the base ambulance and report back here soon as you can."

Bancroft shuffles people away, explaining a gun went off by mistake and the GC is hurt. He gets things somewhat back to normal amidst whispers and conspiracies and returns to Clark's office. He has a ton of questions for Kravchenko who fills him in on the details, that he and the Inspector are working a case related to the GC's suicide and tells him to keep it to himself for the present. Bancroft leaves to meet the ambulance attendants.

Dia has scoured the room and she pulls Kravchenko aside.

"Look. I found this."

Kravchenko sees a heavy cotton sack that Dia has opened to expose a stack of Canadian currency.

"Blackmail, and money. Interesting. Anything else?"

"No. Nothing."

"I think our next move is to get a list of all civilian employees involved in maintenance."

"And we better act fast. Clark said something is happening tonight."

"Right! Let's get a hold of Sergeant Booth as quick as we can. He'll know where we can get the names, or at least who to contact to find out where they keep track of employees. From here on, every minute counts."

58

5:52 pm

Iron Spear is delayed when he reports for work. The guards at the gate are being more thorough, searching all vehicles which enter the base whether they know the occupants or not. The young guard apologizes for having to check his auto because he's known Iron Spear for over a year, seeing him coming and going. He comments on the new car. The lunchbox with the phony thermos is on the front seat and the guard asks him to open it. Trying to hide his nervousness, he keeps it on his knees when he opens it. The guard has a quick glance and waves him through.

Iron Spear parks his car outside the carpenter's shop and moves into position for a speedy withdrawal. He grabs two burlap bags filled with lumber waste in the trunk, acting out the reason he asked to bring the car here. He wants to hurry to the building where he and Emile are working so as to be out of sight. When he's getting into the service truck with his tools and another door to install, one of the plumbers from the shop next door approaches him.

"Hey, Tommy, did you hear the latest gossip?"

"What gossip, Phil?"

"Apparently, the commanding officer accidently shot himself earlier, right in his office."

Iron Spear can't keep the grin off his face. He doesn't have to worry about killing the man any longer. Phil notices the smirk.

"That makes you smile?"

"I didn't like the man. Anytime I was around him, he always had his nose stuck up in the air. Considers us civilians as peons and never said anything nice in my presence. Bet he was probably stealing money or something like that."

Phil nods with a furrowed brow.

"Now that you mention it, he was an arrogant bastard for sure. Well, it's still shocking. And don't tell anyone where you heard it. Supposed to be hush-hush."

"Oh, don't worry. I won't tell anyone. Besides, by now I imagine the rumour mill is running and everybody knows anyway."

"Yeah, likely. Anyway, have a good evening and don't work too hard."

"You too, Phil."

Iron Spear feels like everything is going as planned. Clark's demise only makes him feel more secure. A loose end tied up neatly. He needs to get to the job site. In three hours, he intends to retrieve his gun and knife, kill the electrician, and plant the dynamite. He feels no remorse, only elation which prickles his skin from doing his part for the Reich. Heil Hitler!

59

Kravchenko, Dia and Sergeant Booth are crowded into Flight Sergeant Darrick Kelly's office in the main building. Kravchenko holds a two-page list of employees involved in the maintenance of the base. It's a long list, and Dia sighs at what she feels will be an impossible task to account for everyone before something terrible takes place.

"I don't know, Stefan. That's a long list."

"It is, but with Sergeant Kelly's help we might be able to narrow it down. Do you recognize any or most of these names, Sergeant?"

"Not all of them, but I'm familiar with most of the employees. Many are on the day shift and already left but there might be a few working overtime on the night shift, especially in the heating plant as we are short staffed there at present."

"Ok, let's do it."

Kelly scrutinizes the list and scratches off over forty names. Puts a question mark at the end of thirteen more and gives the list back to Kravchenko. There are twenty-two names left. Three are female. He draws a line through them. They are posted alphabetically. Tommy Wright – carpenter – is listed as a daytime employee and crossed off the list. On a separate sheet of paper, he writes down the first eleven names and gives it to Dia but speaks to Booth.

"Sergeant Booth, will you accompany Inspector Francis to the locale for each of these names. There are parts of the base she is unfamiliar with, and even though she is a police officer, your presence will make her inquiries more official."

"Yes, Sir."

Dia looks at the first name, Samuel Atkins – plumber, and looks askance at Booth.

"We'll have to check into the plumber's shop and find out where he is working. He could be anywhere on base. The night shift, as I understand, usually tackle issues that are non-emergency and when there is no daily traffic."

"Let's get at it then, Sergeant."

"We can take my jeep."

"Jeep? What's a jeep?"

"It's really a Willys quarter ton truck but a two-seater with a fold down windshield. The Americans started calling them jeeps and it stuck. Not sure where the word came from."

"Sounds fine with me. Let's stay in touch, Stefan, and if something comes up, we can contact each other on the walkie-talkies. Don't know how long this will take or what we'll find."

Kravchenko finds the first name on his list is Willie Hutson, a mechanic. He's listed to work in the repair garage.

"Great. Let's get going."

◻

Kravchenko had trouble finding the mechanic. Normally he would be in the garage at his workstation but tonight his supervisor has him working in Hangar Four, unknown to Kravchenko. He checked with the guards at the front gate via walkie-talkie and yes, Hutson came through earlier for his regular shift. One of his co-workers knew he was working on a forklift in one of the hangars but not sure where. When Kravchenko asks the man what Hutson looks like, it fits the description of the man in the parking lot, and Kravchenko makes it a point to find him. By the time he finds him and verifies he is not the person they are looking for, its 8:15 PM. He moves on to the next name – Didier Labrosse - custodian.

Labrosse is easier to find. The custodial office said Labrosse could be found on the first level of the main office building. He and another custodian are polishing the hallway floors. This is fortunate because the other janitor is also on the list – Johan Varney. Kravchenko can eliminate them even without questioning them as their stature doesn't match the image he has of the man in the parking lot. One is taller than Kravchenko and the other much shorter, both as skinny as their mops. Three down and eight to go. 8:49 PM.

Next on his list is Clem Powers – boiler maker - heating plant. When another worker, Daryll Davies, who has been scratched off the list as not possible due to the man's thick glasses, points out Powers, Kravchenko draws a line through the name without even speaking to him. The man is a giant and sports a busy beard. Definitely not the person they seek! The next name is Boris Quinn – electrician. Conveniently enough, the next name, Emile Robichaud, is also an electrician. Kravchenko hopes they're working together to save him some time. As he is making his way to the electrician's shop, he receives a call from Dia via walkie-talkie.

"Stefan. One of our people to check on is Marc-Denis Daigle and when we visited the carpenter's shop, we were told he switched shifts this week with another carpenter, Tommy Wright. Can you add that name to your list? Over."

"Roger that. Will do. Out."

Kravchenko pencils in the name at the bottom of the list. When he arrives at the electrical shop, there is no one around. Scanning copies of work orders, he sees Quinn is installing new heaters in the infirmary and Robichaud's listed as reno in Bldg. No 24. It's not far to the infirmary and Kravchenko leaves his auto at the electrical shop and walks over. Checking his watch under a streetlamp, he sees it is already nine-thirty and everything on base is quiet. When he thinks back to the GC's confirmation of something happening tonight, he feels they have until twelve o'clock. Midnight is what he thinks of as the universal time for evening shenanigans. He hustles along.

He won't get to finish his list.

60

Iron Spear wipes the blood off his knife and replaces it in his coveralls pocket. Large denim pockets. Perfect for hiding his weapons. Dragging the dead body of Emile, the electrician, behind the long rectangular building, he's glad for the cloud cover. He remembers the radio forecasting the chance of rain in the night and hopes it holds off for a while. Dumping the body in the tumble of weeds on the untended back yard which borders the fence on the end, he returns to where he left his lunch box.

Removing the phony thermos, he digs out the stick of dynamite. He already retrieved the blasting cap and fuse. Uniting all elements, he carefully places the explosive in one of the desks in a front office, one of several waiting to be placed back when the work is done. He laughs to himself when he thinks of the mess the explosion will make. He's feeling confidant with his decision and timing. The blast will bring firetrucks and personnel away from his main objective.

He sits in wait, watching for ten o'clock, knowing that many people will be taking breaks and likely be in the mess hall. The only people he thinks he'll need to worry about are the two guards out front, and from his intelligence from Clark, one inside. With any luck, the second guard may be called for backup at the explosion site. After lighting the fuse, he will have enough time to get his truck back to the shop, ready his car and walk to the radio room where the magnetron is.

He's planning on arriving there seconds before the explosion.

One more glance at his watch. 10:00 PM. A buzzing fills his head and he feels a rush, much like a kid on sugar sweets with a new bike to ride. He lights the fuse.

61

Kravchenko is on the opposite side of the base at Hangar Number One where he went to find the second last person on the list – Gerald Urquhart – plumber. He's wrapping up the interview, certain that Urquhart is not the man he's looking for. Heading back out to the auto, he cringes and ducks down when an explosion rips through the air, the noise piercing the quiet of the night. He can see the fireball from where he is and deducts it's near the back of the base. Hustling to his car, he heads toward the flames. He recalls Clark's comment... *tonight.* This is it.

When he's tearing out of the parking lot, Dia comes over the walkie-talkie. He can hardly hear her over the screaming of the sirens and the shrill of the emergency alarm.

"Kravchenko. The blast came from the rear section, farthest building on the street. Booth and I are on our way there. Over.

"Roger. Right behind you. Out."

He tosses the walkie-talkie on the passenger's seat and hastens through the streets as best he can. Other vehicles are stopped and people are gawking and gossiping. He has to wait for the fire trucks to pull out of the station but follows close behind. By the time he reaches the burning building, the fire is lighting up the whole area. Black smoke drifts into the darkness above with embers drifting away, twinkling until they die. Debris is everywhere and the front portion of the building is in complete ruins. Firemen are attaching hoses, grabbing breathing apparatuses and axes. He sees Dia and Booth standing beside the jeep. Their faces are lit up with the wavering light of tall flames. He pulls in behind them. Dia spots him and meets him by his vehicle. The two service police and armed guards work to control the gathering crowd.

"Stefan. This has to be the doing of the killer. But I don't understand why he would target this building, it's empty."

It strikes both of them at the same time. Kravchenko voices their thoughts.

"A divergent. It's meant to create confusion and draw attention away from the other building. Quick, get in. We need to get to the radio station."

There are other vehicles blocking the way out. He has to maneuver the car into the field and back onto the street. People flee and move aside from the oncoming car, spinning dirt from the back wheels. Some wave their fists at what they deem to be reckless driving. Dia is checking her firearm and looks over at Kravchenko. "I hope we're not too late."

62

10:04 pm

Iron Spear parks his car ten feet from the guard shack by the radio building, next to a *No Parking* notice. AC2 Dombrowski scowls at the man. He elbows his buddy and shakes his head.

"Look at that a-hole. Right under the sign. I'll get him on his way. This better be good."

LAC Miller glances out at the man walking across the street, carrying a small toolbox.

"No worries, he works here, a carpenter. He was across the street a few days ago with his truck, fixing one of the back doors on the warehouse. I'll see what he wants. You should do the perimeter, keep your eyes open."

When they step out of the booth, the explosion shocks them into action, what they're trained for. Rifles up, feet braced, they scan the perimeter through the sights of their Enfields. Dombrowski sees the glow out of the corner of his eye.

"What was that? Is the war coming here? Damn."

"Calm down, Dombrowski."

Ignoring the carpenter sprawled out on the skimpy lawn and not sensing any danger, their eyes are drawn to the firelight behind their building, the glow and sparks like a halo over the gable end. Curiosity compels a bunch of people to exit buildings and mingle in speculation. Iron Spear gets up off the dried grass and rights the toolbox he dropped.

The inside guard shouts out from the open doorway.

"Miller, should I go see if I can help?"

"No! Get back inside, Donnie. Stay at your station. No one, I mean no one, gets in."

Iron Spear is three steps behind Miller, dusting off his coveralls. He tries to neglect the pain he feels after falling on his sore arm. It's throbbing. He's being watched by the younger guard whose name tag says Dombrowski, a damn Pollack. Miller is thinking about who's on duty tonight. Twenty armed personnel. Eighteen of them will not leave their posts until ordered to do so. He points a finger at Dombrowski.

"Go there now. LAC Casper with the service police will be there and Lieutenant Pizzarelli. Report to the lieutenant. If you're not needed, come right back here."

Dombrowski hurries off at a full trot. Miller turns his attention to the carpenter. The man is holding a toolbox and tips his head toward the blast.

"What's happening? What's going on?"

"What are you doing here? Civilians have been warned away by your supervisors."

"Yes, of course. My super told me to check with you folks tonight, something about a loose window in the guard shack but never mind, I'll come back after this shit settles down."

Iron Spear appears nonchalant and waves the guard off with a faint smile. Miller looks at the shack then back at Iron Spear.

"I don't remember any window being loose. Who contacted you?"

"I'm not sure. The super would know. I'll come back."

Miller is suspicious now. The man looks shaky."

"Hang on. I'll check with your supervisor."

Iron Spear sets the toolbox down and follows the guard to the shack opening. He doesn't remind the man there is no supervisor on nights, just a list of things to do. As soon as the guard steps in with his back to Iron Spear, he grabs Miller by the neck. In one swift action he reaches over the shoulder and plunges the knife under the sternum upward through the man's heart. He's dead in seconds. Iron Spear looks around to make sure no one is watching, but the action at the blast scene has everyone's attention. After sliding the body down out of sight, Iron Spear takes his toolbox and rushes to the door. Knowing it's locked, he knocks several times until the young lad inside comes to the door. Without opening it, he recognizes the man talking to Miller earlier. He shouts out to Iron Spear.

"What do you want? There is no admittance."

Iron Spear lifts the toolbox up as if it will explain everything and cups his hand around his ear as if he can't hear what the man is saying. LAC Smith opens the door a crack to talk to the intruder and finds the barrel of a handgun jammed into his stomach. Iron Spear pushes the astonished man backward with the barrel of the gun until the door swings closed.

"Do as I say young man and you might live long enough to tell your children this story. One word out of you and you're a dead man. Understand?"

LAC Smith is no hero. He nods vigorously.

"Give me your rifle."

Smith passes his weapon. Iron Spear lays it on the floor and kicks it aside.

"Is there anyone else in the building?"

The radio operator and one other technician in the back."

"Take me to the direction-finding room."

Smith leads Iron Spear down the hallway to the second door on the left. Opening it, he steps into the control room. There are all kinds of radio equipment, lab desks, and in the center is the contraption which Clark told Iron Spear about. Great Britain sent two units under strict secrecy. Only one unit is being used for tests. The second was for back up in the event of failure in the first. It sits on the workbench, still in its original shipping package. The box is marked with an RCAF logo and stamp. Iron spear takes his eyes off the guard for only a swift moment but long enough for Smith to take action.

Smith kicks out at the gun Iron Spear is holding. The weapon flies from Iron Spear's hand with a jolt of pain from his wound. When he slams into the wall, his hand automatically reaches for his knife. Smith is fumbling with the clasp on his side arm. By the time he removes the gun, Iron Spear is on him, the knife in his left hand. Although not ambidextrous, he's still able to wield his weapon. The tip plunges up into the aircraftman's chin. Smith dies instantly.

Iron Spear removes the knife and realizing he doesn't have much time, he retrieves the gun from the floor and listens. Nothing. He checks the hallway, confident that no one heard anything, and hustles away from the room with the knife back in its sheath, the package tightly under his arm. He races to his vehicle and tears away. He has to take the first right, a short jog to the main street, another right and it's straight to the front gate. When he slues around the first turn, Dia and Stefan are almost upon him. They both notice the car they saw at Clark's house which they chased earlier in the day. Iron Spear sees and recognizes them too.

"It's him, Stefan. Turn around, quick."

Iron Spear has to maneuver around cars to get to the front as civilians are being searched and sent home. As he is edging around the third car and with four more in front of him, he sees the approaching vehicle.

"That *verdammt* cop."

He sees an opening on the opposite side of the median. Flooring the accelerator, he forces the car over the concrete curb, across a four-foot section of grass and down onto the opposite side of the street. An armed guard at the gate sees the car rushing toward him and waves with both arms for it to stop. Iron Spear doesn't slow down and barrels into the serviceman, tossing him in the air and off to the side as if he were made of balsa wood. He crashes through the gate, cracking the windshield. Once on the straight stretch toward Highway 134, he guns the car forward. Braking as much as he can, with screeching tires he swerves onto the empty street. There is little traffic on the country road this time of night. Passing through the center of the village, he sees the lights of a pursuing vehicle and curses. Concentrating on the road, he takes the turns and dips as fast as he can, but the other car is still gaining. He desperately needs to get to Cap-de-Cocagne and his dory. The submarine will be surfacing at midnight. He must make the rendezvous. Worrying about the people chasing him, he has an idea.

Two more dead bodies won't make a difference to him.

63

Kravchenko keeps the fleeing car in sight as best as he can. The taillights are visible whenever he comes around a turn or over a rise, and it looks like he's gaining on him. Dia is staring at the road and hanging on.

"Dia, grab the walkie-talkie and get a hold of Booth. Have him contact *HMCS Baffin* and have him warn them of a submarine off the coast near here. That has to be where the culprit is heading. How else would he escape?"

Dia pushes the intercom button and is greeted with static. It takes her a moment to connect with Booth and relay the message. Just as Booth is confirming, the walkie-talkie goes dead.

"I can't tell whether he got the message, Stefan. We're out of range for the radio."

"Let's hope he did. I think we're catching up but he's still quite a way ahead of us."

They loop around Shediac. The escaping vehicle passes the odd other car, often on hills or turns with no thought for oncoming traffic. They are the moves of a desperate man. The red lights of his brakes flash often and sporadically. Kravchenko is driving much too fast and has to brake on the curves, almost losing control several times. Five miles out of Shediac, the car in front of Kravchenko bears to the right.

"I don't know this part of the country, Dia. Where could he be going?"

"I think that's the cut off for Cap-de-Cocagne. It would make sense if he were meeting a submarine. It juts out into the bay with lots of beaches and a few cottages. Mostly farmers and fishermen live along there. He must have a boat stored somewhere for his escape."

"We'd better hope we catch up to him before he does. I have no idea where we would find a boat. We'd lose him then."

"Can't this car go faster?"

"Probably, but I'm going as fast as I dare. I'm not a stunt driver. Damn, I've lost him."

Dia has been eyeing the car and is familiar with the terrain enough to know the road along the shore makes a wide circular sweep of the isthmus. It runs through a wooded section, sparse forest on each side.

"No, he's just in the turn. It's a long stretch around the head of the land. Listen, Stefan, if he's making a meet with the submarine, his escape has to be near here. Slow down."

His foot comes off the accelerator, more in surprise than in response to her command. He looks across to her with a scrunched look.

"Slow down?"

"Yes. He has to pick up a boat somewhere if that's what he's doing. I feel that's safe to assume so. His escape route must be close in the wooded stretch ahead. This is as far out into the bay as the land goes. It only makes sense. Don't you agree?"

He slows to a horse's trot and kills the lights.

"You're right. How far is the wooded part?"

Dia is adjusting her night vision. The clouds which have been nagging them all day are breaking up. Intermittent starlight sharpens the shadows. She studies the driver's side of the road for trails or tire marks.

"I'm not sure but it takes a couple of minutes to drive to the next clearing. You can go a little faster. He would head toward the shore on your side."

Kravchenko is carefully driving in the dark. He can make out the edge of the road on both sides and keep the car in the center, sitting back so Dia can see out his window.

"Hey, watch it. Slow down."

"Yeah, yeah sorry. It's not easy to see. No moon, just a few stars sometimes. Besides' it's your fault."

"My fault?"

"Yeah, the perfume, it's quite pleasant and um... anyway, it's nice and it suits you.

"Yeah, well, listen here, Kravchenko, we're not on a date, so pay attention. Go a little faster."

"What if we're wrong, Dia, and he's long gone?"

She pats him on the shoulder.

"Trust me on this, Stefan, this seems right. I can feel it."

64

11:08 pm

Iron Spear had doused his lights when he was out of view of the car behind him. Knowing the road by memory, he's soon at the cut-off for the cottage and pulls the car right up to the back of the house. Grabbing the box from the passenger's seat, he's surprised how such a small thing can be of so much importance. Not his to ask. Checking his gun, he gets out of the car and hustles toward the beach. His sore arm hurts from using it so much. He stops to dry mouth two more painkillers. He can shoot left-handed if he has to. But he hopes the people after him have gone by. They can't know where he was going.

He doesn't have time to worry, just get on the water. As many times as he's walked the route to the edge of the property, it's difficult to see tonight. The dead grass is longer and twisted together in places and he stumbles several times. When he reaches the edge of the property, there is cliff as tall as he is along most of the shore. To the left the land dips close to the property line. From there a set of rickety stairs with four steps reaches a stretch of fine sand. He clutches the package and makes his way down by holding a rail. His dory is not far, tethered to a dead root sticking out of the cliff. With the tide almost full, he only has to drag it half a dozen steps to the water.

Placing the package in the bottom, he has trouble untying the knot he secured it with and has to dig out his knife. When he reaches for the length of rope, a beam of light appears over the top of the cliff. A car.

Trying to remain calm, he hurries to cut the rope. He can hear voices. Leaving the dory, he scrambles back to the stairs and lowering himself, peers over the top lip. Someone is running toward him, only a silhouette in the beam of the car lights. Raising his gun, he aims at the figure's torso and fires. The figure falls.

Time to flee.

65

Dia stares at the edge of the road and they come upon an open area, a driveway. Tires tracks disturb the dirt.

"Stop, Stefan. Look, tire tracks. I think there is a house to the left. It's hard to see but turn in."

"All right. I see it."

When they turn in, the car headlights sweep over the property, and they can see the reflections off the water. Driving in slowly, Kravchenko points out the shrubs which have been run over.

"Look there, Dia, car tracks look fresh."

"Yes, and there's the car in the back yard. Looks like he was trying to hide it. He must've headed for the water and a boat. Let's go see."

He puts the car in neutral and sets the emergency brake. Getting out he checks the surroundings looking for any danger. Removing his sidearm, he points to the back of the house where the car is.

"Check around the building Dia. Be careful. I'm going to the shore."

Dia walks around the edge of the house with her gun raised in two hands. Standing at the car she touches the hood.

"Better hurry, Stefan. He hasn't been here too long. The hood is still warm."

Kravchenko hastens toward the shore when a shot rings out. Whatever angels are protecting Kravchenko, they're paying attention. The bullet takes off a chunk of skin from the top of his right ear. The reaction knocks him to the ground and sends his hat and gun up in the air. Dia returns fire where she saw the gun flash. She's rewarded with a grunt and a curse. She runs to their auto to douse the lights then heads back to where she saw Kravchenko fall, her voice filled with concern.

"Stefan, are you okay? Answer me."

"No...no, I'm not. Give me a minute."

Holding his hand to his ear, he quickly jerks it away at the stinging wound. He can feel the slippery presence of blood on his fingers. Pulling his handkerchief from his trouser pocket, he rolls it like a bandanna and wraps it around his head covering the ear, and ties a knot to hold it in place. He stands up and Dia turns toward the water.

"I hear something being dragged on the sand. Are you good?"

"That was too close. We need to stop him, but I can't find my gun. It's too dark."

"Never mind, I have mine. I think I hit him. Let's go."

Dia gets to the edge of the cliff and crouches down so she won't be a target. She sees movement on the water, but she can't make out any details, only the bobbing of a night shadow. She shoots at the center of the action. Kravchenko is on his knees beside her. They both duck as the shots are returned. A loud noise farther out startles them. Looking out into the bay, they see something rise out of the water. Clouds scud across the sky and when they open up, starlight reveals a dark silhouette. Kravchenko nudges his partner.

"It's the submarine. We can't let him make it."

"What can we do? I can't even see him anymore."

"I don't know. Let's get to the beach and maybe there is another boat nearby."

"I doubt it. There aren't even any houses nearby. Be careful, we're at the edge of a cliff."

"There must be a way down somewhere."

They can make out the slope of the terrain away from their left and follow the field until the image of a stairway appears. Rushing down the steps, they run up the beach to where the figure of a boat and the movement of oars is moving away from them. Dia points to shadows in front of the sub.

"There. He's still a ways from the submarine."

Kravchenko is about to reply when off to the east a broad light sweeps around the eastern tip of the isthmus. The thunder of a ship at full throttle reaches them the same time as it reaches Iron Spear. He's rowing as fast as he can with an injured arm and a shoulder which burns where a bullet grazed the muscle. Biting down on the pain, he's frantic, rowing erratically. A powerful beam of the light catches the sub broadside. A siren from within the submarine shrills into the emptiness around them. There are sailors on the deck maneuvering a large machine gun, shooting at the light which is bearing down on them. Return fire comes from the ship. One of the men on the submarine goes down and flops into the water. Another man takes over and hits the light on the ship but the ship keeps a direct path to the sub.

Less than twenty seconds go by with gunfire cutting the night and the ship rams the sub astern of the conning tower. The heavy prow of the sub hunter is reinforced and screeches against the metal of the sub, piercing the top which sits a foot out of the water. The heavy engines don't stop, driving the sub downward. Another bright light from the ship flashes on the sub. Men are shooting from the top of the conning tower. Returning shots take them out.

Kravchenko can see the man in the boat in the peripheral glow of the lights sitting idle staring at the duel of sea crafts.

"It's the *Baffin*, Dia. Booth must've gotten a hold of them, and they were patrolling close by. And the man in the boat has a front row seat. Look out he's pointing his gun this way."

In desperation, Iron Spear shoots back at the silhouettes.

Dia kneels on the soft sand digging her knees and foot in, both hands on her service revolver. She lines up the man's torso, a black blotch in the glare of the searchlight. No wind. One shot. It pierces Iron Spear in the lower left lung and escapes through the heart. The body totters forward. Wavelets from the dueling boats make it tip overboard.

Kravchenko is awed by the shot.

"Good hit. You must practice."

"I do."

Dusting the sand from her knees, she notices Kravchenko step closer to the water, watching the ships offshore.

"What's happening out there?"

As if in answer, gunfire breaks out. Men appear on the conning tower but are soon picked off by sharpshooters from the ship.

"Look Dia, the nose of the sub in sinking. The *Baffin* is backing off."

66

When the *Baffin* strikes U-boat 498, *Oberleutnant Zur See* Atzinger was in the control room, readying the boat for full submergence so he could hasten out of the bay. There was little warning, only by visual sight from the executive officer on the conning tower. He ordered men to the deck guns. He can't submerge until Iron Spear is aboard.

The impact sends men sprawling, falling to the floor. The sub is nose downward and swinging to port. He is aft of the rip in the metal and engineers are reporting heavy damage with water filling the torpedo chamber. He hears the screeching of metal on metal as the ship tries to lose itself from the sub. The sub starts swinging to starboard. Engines are idling and Atzinger's first thought is to save the sub and his crew. He orders more men to the conning tower but they are met with heavy gun fire. When more men attempt to close it, they too are gunned down. He can feel the nose dropping. He orders full ahead, come to 130 degrees. It's his only chance.

The Canadian sailors abandoned the conning tower under orders from *the HMCS Baffin*. The ship backs off five hundred feet and readies the 12-pounder naval cannon. Three rapid shots blow holes in the side of the submarine large enough for a man to crawl through. Large enough for gallons of water to gush in. Ten crew members die immediately. The rest of the crew will drown as U-boat 498 sinks to the seabed in the Northumberland Strait.

◻

The body of Manfred Becker, aka Iron Spear, aka Tommy Wright, is picked up by the *Baffin*.

The magnetron is retrieved from the dory and returned to RCAF Station Scoudouc.

The body of Group Captain Braydon Clark will be returned to family in Moosejaw, Saskatchewan with a citation he died in the line of duty with the file sealed.

Oberstleutnant Dieter Schmitz will be demoted and transferred to the German Army and sent to Russia in preparation for Operation Typhoon, a major offensive action toward Moscow. He will be killed by a Russian sniper three days after his arrival.

Aircraftsman 2 Jeremy Carter will bypass Aircraftsman 1 to be promoted to a Leading Aircraftsman. He will recover fully in three weeks and be back on duty at RCAF Station Scoudouc.

Flight Sergeant Wilbur Booth will be promoted to Warrant Officer.

67

Wednesday, October 15th 5:25 pm

Stefan Kravchenko is not in uniform. He is dressed instead in navy dress pants, white shirt with a dark blue and white striped tie, shoes that shine like headlights, waist length leather coat and a brand-new fedora which hides the small bandage on his ear. He stands in front of the house on Gordon Street in Moncton. In one hand is a tinsel wrapped bouquet of six red sweetheart roses. The other hand presses the doorbell. He has to wait several minutes before it is answered.

When the door opens he's greeted by a smile which makes his heart pick up a pace. Dia Francis wears a soft green dress, cinched at the narrow waist with a white belt. Her hat is simple, a matching green with a wide brim. Her beige wool coat falls below the hemline at the knees. The boots are dainty and shine like Kravchenko's. Her face is bright with anticipation.

"You're right on time, Stefan. And the flowers are beautiful. Thank you."

"Of course. Do you think I would miss the opportunity of having dinner with the most beautiful woman I've ever met?"

"Oh, you flatterer you. I love it. Now where are you taking me?"

"I understand that Cy's Seafood on High Street is quite good. And after that High Sierra with Humphrey Bogart and Ida Lupino is playing at the Empress theatre. Do you like Bogart?"

"Yes, I do. Sounds like fun. Let me put these roses in a vase and I'll be ready in a jiffy."

In a few moments, Kravchenko escorts Dia to his auto and opens the door for her.

"A real gentleman too. You keep this up, Warrant Officer Kravchenko, and I might get to like you even more than I already do."

"That's the plan."

The End

During my research for locations used in New Brunswick during the second world war, I came across Air Force Station Scoudouc. What caught my attention was the addition of the No. 1 Radio Direction Finding Maintenance Unit added to the base in 1941. (No.1 RFD MU) Along with it, came secrets.

I've not been able to discover what the secrets may have been so I used the magnetron as the secret to protect in my story.

It's all made up, of course. The base actually existed as you can see from the photo above but I've rearranged buildings and personnel to fit my tale.

I want to thank those who have helped me get to a finished book.

My lovely wife, Gloria. My family. Special friends, Gracia & Allen.

To Sandra Bunting for her fine editing skills.

Steve Chiasson, formatter extraordinaire.

Charming and valuable beta readers Author Angela Wren and Gail Brown.

To CWO (ret) Terry J Beers CD, for military matters.

Donna Dean for a great cover.

Author MJ LaBeff for continuing and encouraging support.

There are many to thank and not enough space, who share my news on social media and I appreciate all you do.

Thank you dear reader for reading and buying my book. It's been a labour of love especially with you in mind.

About the Author

Growing up in South Branch, Allan Hudson was encouraged to read from an early age by his mother who was a schoolteacher. He lives in Dieppe, NB, with his wife Gloria. He has enjoyed a lifetime of adventure, travel and uses the many experiences as ideas for his writing. He is an author of action/adventure novels, historical fiction and a short story collection. His short stories – The Ship Breakers & In the Abyss – received Honourable Mention in the New Brunswick Writer's Federation competition.

He contributes to an anthology with eight other authors.

He has stories published on commuterlit.com, The Golden Ratio and his blog - South Branch Scribbler.

www.southbranchscribbler.com